Dearly Despised

(Calluvia's Royalty Book 5)

Alessandra Hazard

Copyright © 2022 Alessandra Hazard

ISBN: 9798829838232

This book contains steamy M/M content and graphic language. For mature audiences only.

Table of Contents

Chapter 1

"You will be the king when you grow up."

Those were the first words his mother said that morning.

Samir was five. His sleepy mind couldn't understand what she was saying.

"They're gone, my darling," his mother said.

Samir blinked, utterly confused. Was Mother talking about the king and queen-consort? They had died months ago.

"Not them," his mother said, with a strange smile. "The princes. Warrehn and little Eri. They were kidnapped by the rebels." She added after a moment, "Poor things. They're almost certainly dead."

Samir stared at her.

Despite being a child, even he could tell she wasn't being honest. His mother was glad that Warrehn and baby Eri were gone.

Samir wasn't glad, but he wasn't upset, either. He simply didn't know them well. Warrehn was a lot older than him—ten—so he had never played with Samir. Eri was just three—he was practically a *baby*—so he and Samir didn't really play together, either. Besides, there was the fact that Samir and his mother were basically the poor relations. Samir was technically next in line for the throne after the princes, but he came from a secondary royal line that descended from a completely different branch of the royal family tree, so distantly related to the royal family that they might as well not be related at all. The House of Zaver and the House of Lavette had shared a common ancestor eight hundred years ago. Samir was never supposed to inherit.

But he would, if the princes really were dead.

Three months later, the Council of Twelve Grand Clans declared that Prince Warrehn and Prince Eruadarhd were likely dead and named Samir the heir presumptive. His mother was to be his regent until he turned twenty-five.

In the following few days, everyone who was anyone seemed to remark on it. *Such a tragedy*, people exclaimed loudly before whispering to Samir's mother, *Such luck for your son, my dear.*

Luck. Samir supposed that from a certain point of view it really was an insane stroke of luck that he, an insignificant prince from a secondary royal line, had been elevated to the status of a future king. His mother was *thrilled*, and it made Samir feel a little weird. He loved the large playroom in the royal palace, loved the expensive, amazing toys he suddenly owned, but he couldn't help but feel like he and his mother didn't really own them. Like they'd stolen them.

But as years passed, that feeling slowly went away.

He was Samir'ngh'lavette, the future king of the Fifth Grand Clan.

That was how he was raised.

That was who he was for nearly twenty years.

Until he suddenly wasn't.

***

Apparently Prince Warrehn wasn't dead.

And he was coming back home.

"This cannot be happening," Dalatteya muttered under her breath, pacing the throne room. "A solution. There has to be a solution!"

Samir watched his mother, a strange sort of numbness filling his insides ever since he had heard the news. "He's the rightful king, Mother," he stated. He felt… off-balance. As if everything he knew about his world had been turned upside down. Just a few hours ago he had been preparing for his upcoming coronation. He was to be the king when he turned twenty-five, the position his mother had groomed him for since he was five. In fact, he was practically the king already, ruling their grand clan through his mother, who was his regent. But now he was back to being the poor relation. No one.

It was surreal.

Dalatteya glared at him. "Stop talking nonsense, Samir!" she bit out. "You're the rightful king, not him! He isn't the one who made our grand clan the most prosperous on the planet!" Her beautiful face brightened, her dark blue eyes becoming calculating. "We can use it, in fact. Our people love you, not him. All Warrehn has going for him is his lineage. It won't be impossible to overthrow him."

"Mother," Samir said, glancing around. That kind of talk was dangerous.

But Dalatteya ignored him and resumed pacing, muttering something under her breath.

Samir sighed, watching her twirl a lock of her violet hair as she thought. He loved his mother, he truly did, but she could be a little too much sometimes.

He didn't like seeing her like this. He had known she could be ruthless and calculating, but it was usually for a good reason. This... he wasn't sure it was a good one. While he did feel upset at his life being overturned again, Samir didn't feel like he was entitled to the throne the way his mother seemed to think he should be. Warrehn had been the crown prince as a ten-year-old; he was of age now, twenty-nine, almost thirty. He was the rightful king of the Fifth Grand Clan by right of succession. Samir would have to accept it.

It would be a lie to say that he didn't feel any resentment or disappointment. He did. Of course he did. After fifteen years of preparing for the role and effectively ruling for the past four years, he felt... robbed. Completely blindsided. As if his life suddenly had no meaning or purpose. If he wasn't the future king, who was he? It had been part of his identity for most of his life. So yes, he was disappointed and upset. But it was nothing compared to the sheer rage emanating from his mother.

"Mother, calm down," Samir said. "There is nothing we can do. If Warrehn is truly alive, there's nothing we can do but graciously step down. The throne is his by right."

"You don't understand," she snapped, agitation rolling off her in waves. "After everything I've done—he can't just come back and take it all away."

Samir frowned.

"What... What do you mean?"

She said nothing, her expression becoming impossible to read.

Samir had always envied her this ability. While he looked a lot like his mother, having inherited her violet hair, pale skin, and dark blue eyes, he hadn't inherited her ability to flawlessly hide her thoughts when she wanted to.

"I mean that I've put so much effort into making you the best possible king for this country," she said at last. "Twenty years, wasted. No, I refuse to take it lying down."

Samir felt a pang of pity for her. The news had probably been a bigger blow for his mother than it had been for him. She'd always wanted to see him on the throne; she had been so invested in it—had always been so invested in *him*. Samir knew everything his mother did was for him. Despite her rare beauty, she hadn't remarried after being widowed, even though she'd never lacked admirers. She had ignored the numerous off-worlders and widowed Calluvians who had courted her for years, spending all her time on her only son, teaching him politics and languages and getting him the best tutors in areas she wasn't qualified to teach. Samir knew how lucky he was to have such a supportive mother. In most royal families, parents were nowhere near as involved in their children's education and upbringing. He had the best mother in the world. He was more upset on her behalf than his own.

"Mother," Samir said in a placating tone, getting to his feet and taking her delicate hands into his. "I know you're upset, but please be careful of what you're saying. People might overhear and *misunderstand* you."

Dalatteya gave him a long look, something cold and calculating about her expression. "Misunderstand me? There's no misunderstanding, Samir. I will not see anyone but my son on the throne of this country. That's the end of the matter."

Samir stared at her, and she stared right back.

A sinking feeling appeared in the pit of his stomach. Looking at her now, Samir could no longer push back the thought that had kept resurfacing from time to time—the thought that she might have had something to do with the princes' disappearance.

"Don't look at me that way," she said after a long, thick silence. "I did what I had to."

Samir covered his eyes with his hand and shook his head, unable to believe what he was hearing. He wasn't naive. Nor was he foolishly idealistic. He knew that sometimes it was necessary to be ruthless in politics. But doing something to *children*… he drew the line there.

"I can't believe you," he whispered harshly. "They were kids—the youngest prince was three!"

Dalatteya sighed. "I know," she said, her voice wavering before becoming firm again. "I'm not proud of it. But what's done is done. Now we have to deal with the consequences. Warrehn likely suspects that I'm behind the assassination attempt on him and his brother."

Samir shook his head, unable to believe how flippant she was being. "*Three*, Mother! You're to blame for the death of a toddler!"

"Yes, I had to make some hard decisions, but everything I did was for you!"

Samir gaped. "You can't just use that as an excuse—"

"You ungrateful, foolish boy," she hissed out, her eyes glistening with tears. "Do you already not remember the way we were treated before? Like poor relations, barely tolerated for the sake of appearances? They looked down on us, sneered at us, and the queen-consort hated me—and you by association."

Samir frowned. He did recall that, actually. Even as a child, it was hard to miss the strong dislike the queen-consort emanated around his mother. He'd never found out why—it hadn't interested him much as a child—and the queen-consort was already dead by the time he was curious enough about such adult matters. He only knew that his mother and the late king had grown up together after Dalatteya had been adopted into the House of Zaver after losing her parents.

"Why?" he said. "Why did she hate you?"

Dalatteya pursed her lips and took a moment to reply. "Emyr—the king was fixated on me. The queen-consort was mad with jealousy, even though her husband's obsession was hardly my fault. I certainly didn't encourage him."

Samir's brows drew together. Now that he thought of it, he vaguely recalled coming across his mother and King Emyr arguing heatedly; he'd once seen him grabbing Dalatteya's arm and refusing to let go when Samir walked into the room. As a young boy, he hadn't thought much of it, but as an adult… he couldn't believe that he hadn't put two and two together until now.

"Was his marriage bond to the queen-consort faulty, then?" Samir said, referring to the fact that generally bondmates were incapable of feeling much of an attraction to anyone other than their spouses.

Dalatteya gave a shrug, her face terribly blank in a way that told Samir that she was hiding some strong emotion.

"His telepathy had become erratic after he fell off a zywern and hit his head when he was a boy," she said in a toneless voice. "All his telepathic bonds were very weak, including his marriage one. He never cared for his betrothed and spent all his youth chasing after me, even though I was betrothed to your father and married him eventually." Her lips thinned. "The king killed him, you know."

Samir whispered, "What?"

"It was Emyr who had your father murdered; it wasn't the muggers. Emyr hated him, hated that your father touched what he considered his."

What he considered his?

Samir went cold. "Mother, did King Emyr—did he force you…?"

Avoiding his eyes, Dalatteya laughed, the sound sharp and broken. "You don't say no to a king, Samir."

Samir sprang to his feet and started pacing, feeling sick to his stomach.

Gods.

So many things made sense now: the way the king had kept them in the palace, even though they were members of a different House, the fact that the queen-consort had hated his mother, and the fact that his mother had looked pale and haunted after his father's death… The way Dalatteya had looked almost *relieved* when the royal couple had died in the terrorist attack.

The terrorist attack.

Samir came to an abrupt halt, his back to his mother. "It wasn't a terrorist attack, was it?"

There was only silence in response.

At long last, his mother spoke, her voice so toneless and quiet it was barely audible. "I was sixteen when it happened the first time. I endured being the subject of his sick obsession for twenty-three years, Samir. I endured his wife's hatred for as long. But him killing my husband was the last straw. I couldn't bear letting your father's killer touch my body. So I killed him. The day he died, I was finally free."

Samir inhaled shakily, not sure what to think. He definitely understood why his mother had done it, and he very much empathized with her, but…

"Did you intend for the queen-consort to die, too?" he said, hoping desperately that she'd say no, that she'd say that the queen-consort had been collateral damage.

"Yes," Dalatteya said in the same toneless voice. "I had to. The moment Emyr died, she would have had us both killed. She had attempted to poison me twice, and nearly killed you when you tried my food. You probably don't remember it—you were just three. She hated me, Samir. That kind of hatred doesn't go away. I had to protect us. She had to die too."

Samir closed his eyes. "What about their children? They were innocent."

She sighed. "I'm not a monster. I didn't intend to do anything to them at first. But I knew they'd become suspicious of what happened to their parents when they grew up—and then they might find out the truth. Warrehn was already starting to ask questions about the terrorist attack. I had no choice. Besides…"

When she trailed off and didn't say anything else, Samir turned and looked at her.

There was a strange, mad sort of fire in Dalatteya's eyes as she said, "It was my revenge too. I knew *he* would hate the fact that you, the son of the man he hated, the boy whose existence he hated, would inherit his throne instead of his own flesh and blood. And he hates it, I know he hates it so much."

Samir stared at her before saying slowly, "King Emyr is dead, Mother. You do realize that, right?"

Dalatteya blinked, as if waking up from a dream. She scowled, her lips pursing tightly, before looking away. "Of course I know that—I'm not insane."

Samir nodded, not really convinced. He suddenly wondered if Emyr's obsession had been entirely one-sided.

After all, it was possible to be obsessed with a man you hated and despised. People said losing someone one hated passionately was as difficult as losing someone one loved—and as difficult to move on from.

Pushing the thought away to examine later, Samir focused on a more pressing issue. "But apparently Prince Warrehn isn't dead, after all. What happened, Mother?"

Dalatteya stroked her lips thoughtfully. She truly was still an exquisitely beautiful woman, Samir noted objectively. She was fifty-nine, middle-aged by Calluvian standards, but she still outshone most young women. It was no wonder King Emyr had been so obsessed with her despite his own wife being a golden-haired beauty. Although Samir looked like her, he'd always felt like he was just a poor imitation of his mother. A pretty good fake that didn't have her ethereal appearance.

"I'm not entirely sure what happened," she said. "I bribed the princes' bodyguards to dispose of the boys and I'm not sure I trust their account of what happened. They were supposed to kill them in the forest and blame it on the rebels. But somehow, the boys escaped. I understand there was a chase and the youngest prince died in the chaos."

Dalatteya shook her head with a wince, rubbing at her temples. "Poor thing. I truly didn't want to harm him, but at the time I thought I had no other choice. I probably wouldn't make the same choice now—little Eri was innocent, and I've always been very fond of him, even though he was *his* spawn—but back then, I simply panicked and acted when Warrehn started asking questions."

Samir looked at her searchingly. "What about Warrehn?"

A faint grimace touched Dalatteya's lips.

"In an ironic twist of fate, it appears the rebels truly were in the area, and they kidnapped him. Warrehn somehow ended up on a remote colony of the Third Grand Clan, Tai'Lehr, and has been living there as a reluctant guest all these years. I found out about it with the rest of the Council—I truly thought that he was dead until then."

Samir sighed. He didn't know what to think. How to feel. Objectively, he understood why his mother had done it, and even subjectively, he had no issue with her killing the man who had sexually coerced her for years and killed Samir's father. But the princes… He was more conflicted about it. Rationally, he felt disgusted by her ruthlessness toward children, yet he still couldn't hate her. She was his mother. He loved her, despite everything. She was his *mother*. He would die for her.

"All right," he said. There was no point in dwelling on her past choices and mistakes. They had to deal with the consequences now. That was more important. "Can Warrehn prove your involvement in his parents' deaths?"

"No," Dalatteya said confidently. "I've made sure to erase all the evidence in the years since then. Nothing can be traced back to me now."

Suppressing the urge to snap that she should have simply done that instead of panicking when Warrehn had started asking questions and deciding to dispose of him, Samir took a deep breath and said in an even voice, "All right. What about the attack on the princes? Can he prove that you were involved?"

Dalatteya chewed on her lip, her eyes narrowed in thought.

"I do not know," she said quietly. "It's possible that he overheard his bodyguards and that's why he bolted. I don't know what he might have overheard."

"Great," Samir muttered under his breath, heaving a sigh and running a hand over his face.

"It doesn't signify," his mother said. "He will have to die."

Samir lifted his head and stared at her.

She stared back calmly.

Chapter 2

There was a real possibility that his mother was a little insane.

There was a real possibility that Samir was insane too, because he was humoring her. For the time being. Or at least that was what he told himself. He was humoring her insane idea to get rid of Warrehn—kill the rightful king—until Samir could come up with a better solution.

Was there a better solution though? He had to work with the hand he'd been dealt, and that hand was terrible. He didn't want his mother to be arrested. He had to protect her. She might have been misguided in her actions, but he knew she meant well, even if her sense of justice was extremely lopsided. Or maybe he just couldn't be objective about her. She was his mother, his only family.

"Don't do anything rash, Mother," Samir said, keeping a pleasant smile on his face as he and Dalatteya stood by the main entrance to their palace.

Warrehn's palace, he corrected himself mentally.

"Of course not, my dear," his mother said, her slim hand resting on his bicep. Her face was a perfectly pleasant mask that likely fooled all the nobles surrounding them. All of them were watching them like hawks—or rather, like vipers looking for some juicy gossip.

Samir was determined not to give them anything to talk about.

He kept his expression neutral as the aircar landed on the front lawn.

The man who emerged out of it was tall. That was the first thing Samir registered. He was very tall and muscular, making everyone else look short in comparison. The man's hair glimmered bronze in the early sunlight, but Samir had a feeling it would look more brown in other circumstances.

He studied the man's face curiously. He had trouble seeing the easy-going ten-year-old boy he remembered in that grim man with hard blue eyes. He was handsome, Samir supposed, or he would be if he weren't frowning so much. He looked distinctly unhappy as he surveyed the small crowd gathered to greet him before his heavy gaze finally fell on Samir and his mother.

His eyes sharpened, his face somehow becoming harder. He glowered at them, his telepathic presence emanating strong dislike, loud and clear.

Samir's practiced smile froze on his lips. He glanced at his mother for guidance, but Dalatteya's face betrayed nothing. Unlike Samir, she held Warrehn's gaze unflinchingly, radiating polite indifference, like a queen deigning to speak to someone far beneath her.

"Nephew," she said, smiling.

All the whispers ceased as everyone waited for Warrehn's reaction.

"You're not my aunt," Warrehn said, his voice as hard as his face.

Samir blinked, still stunned by his attitude. He had thought Warrehn would at least keep the pretense of politeness. All the royals did, regardless of their personal feelings. It was just the way things were *done*. No one said what they actually thought in court. Except for Warrehn, apparently.

Dalatteya's smile turned cloyingly sweet. "I know I'm not your aunt by blood, my dear, but you did call me Auntie when you were a boy. I'd like you to keep calling me that."

Warrehn stared her down. "And I'd like you to move out of my house, *Auntie*."

A ripple of scandalized whispers broke through the crowd.

Dalatteya's smile froze. For the first time, she looked unsure, clearly thrown off balance by Warrehn's attitude, before her eyes narrowed, a dangerous glint appearing in them.

Samir frowned. There were two ways this could go: things would escalate to a full-on civil war, or he needed to somehow break the tension and calm everyone down, and fast, before the gossip spread.

So he stepped forward, smiling, and walked over to Warrehn.

"I've missed your sense of humor!" he said, raising his voice just enough to be heard, and hugged him.

It was like hugging a statue. Or rather, something made of durasteel. Warrehn was rigid against him, his telepathic presence like a live wire. He really was very tall and broad, making Samir feel small—and he was very far from being small.

A few seconds passed.

Then, Warrehn none too gently pushed him away and glowered at him, with a mix of bewilderment and obvious dislike in his gaze. "What the—"

"I know, you look so different from how I remember you, too!" Samir cut him off, beaming at him. "But I'd recognize your awful sense of humor anywhere!"

Warrehn glared at him. "I don't—"

"Let's go, I'll show you your room," Samir said, grabbing his hand and all but dragging him toward the front door, away from the curious eyes and gossipmongers. The guards by the front door bowed to them, their impassive faces a stark contrast to the curiosity they emanated.

Samir dragged Warrehn into the nearest room. He shut the door and dropped his smile as soon as they were alone. "Are you out of your mind?" he said, turning to Warrehn. "I don't care about your issues with my mother, but you shouldn't talk that way to her in front of the entire court! You'll just make all of us the subject of nasty gossip."

"What makes you think I care?" Warrehn said in a flat voice.

Samir opened his mouth and closed it without saying anything, looking at the older man in silence, at a loss for words. He'd never met a member of royalty who didn't care about their reputation and public image.

Warrehn's lips twisted. It was kind of amazing how such an objectively handsome man could look so unattractive. Warrehn's features were classically handsome, but the deep frown between his finely shaped brows and around his mouth made him look almost ugly. His thick, slightly curly honey-brown hair was the only soft thing about him, his jaw hard and square and dusted with dark stubble. Blue eyes glared at Samir with such derision it was a little unnerving—and Samir wasn't an easily unnerved man.

"I can't stand politicians, liars, and traitors," Warrehn said in the same toneless, gruff voice. "And you and your mother are all of those things."

So that answered the question of whether Warrehn suspected the truth or not.

Warrehn stepped closer, looming over him. "I can't prove your guilt—yet—but I want you out of my sight. Out of my house."

Samir lifted his chin, his heart beating so fast it nearly made him dizzy. "I don't know what you're implying. If you're trying to imply that I was somehow involved in the attack on you, let me remind you that I was *five* at the time."

"You were," Warrehn said, looking him in the eyes with the same hard expression, radiating dislike. "I'm sure it wasn't your idea at the time. But you've been more than content to benefit from your mother's treachery as you sat on my throne, spent my money, and slept in my bed."

Samir flushed. "I didn't sleep in your bed," he bit out, more bothered by Warrehn's words than he would have liked.

"You know perfectly well what I mean."

Samir pressed his lips together, hating that he couldn't refute it. No matter how hard he had tried to justify his mother's actions, his inner sense of fairness and conscience didn't approve of them. But he couldn't exactly say it.

"My mother is innocent," he said at last, belatedly remembering that he had to keep up appearances. There were ways to extract memories and show them to the authorities. While memories were rarely considered ultimate proof of one's guilt or innocence, if there were enough of them accumulated, they could do a lot of damage, at least to one's reputation.

Warrehn smiled grimly. "Don't waste your breath. I know the truth. It's only a matter of time before everyone else does—and you and your traitorous cunt of a mother end up where you belong."

"Don't talk about my mother that way."

"What way?" Warrehn said, raising his eyebrows. "Since when is telling the truth offensive? She's a cunt and a traitor. I wouldn't be surprised if she got where she is by using her cunt, too. It's not like she had much else to pay with for betraying us."

Samir punched him hard telepathically, but the bastard didn't even flinch, his mental shields like an impenetrable wall. It only infuriated Samir more. "Don't you dare speak of my mother like that," he hissed, breathing hard. His fingers were shaking so badly he had to curl them into fists. At moments like this, he wished he were good at hand-to-hand combat. He wanted to *shut Warrehn up*, but he didn't know how. He'd never felt more powerless in his life.

"Or what?" Warrehn said with a sardonic glint in his eye. "You'll have me murdered? Your *cunt* of a mother already tried that."

Samir punched him in the jaw — or rather, he tried. A hand grabbed his wrist in a punishing grip, and then Warrehn shoved his arm against the door, pinning it to it, and loomed over him.

"You don't get to play righteous indignation when you and your mother have built your lives on the bones of my family," Warrehn said, his blue eyes steely, his breath brushing against Samir's face. "She killed my parents. She killed my brother — a toddler. There's no redemption for the likes of you. A 'cunt' is too kind a word for the likes of you."

We had nothing to do with their deaths.

That was what Samir should have said. But he was rendered speechless, unable to speak under the crushing weight of Warrehn's hatred.

He could feel that hatred with his skin: hot, relentless, and unstoppable. This man hated him. Truly hated him. Abhorred him. And nothing would ever change that, no matter what Samir said in his defense. In Warrehn's eyes, Samir was as complicit in his family's deaths as Dalatteya was, because he was the one who had benefited from them.

"I'm sorry for your loss," Samir said softly.

Warrehn shot him a disgusted look and, shoving him away, stalked out of the room.

Samir sagged against the wall and closed his eyes, still shivering and feeling like he'd just been run over by a large, unstoppable force. It felt strange to be hated, and hated with such intensity. People normally loved him. Not that they really knew him, but they loved him. He was used to being loved.

Being hated… it had shaken him to his core. He felt odd. Wrong-footed.

Like a different person entirely.

Chapter 3

"No, did you see that? The way that boy strutted around, like he owned the place?"

Samir said nothing, listlessly poking the food on his plate with his fork. He didn't bother telling his mother that Warrehn did own the place. Technically, even the plate Samir was staring at belonged to Warrehn, not them. But he knew his mother wouldn't listen. So he remained silent.

Ever since the encounter with Warrehn a few hours ago, he felt off-balance and shaken. Torn between fury and guilt. It was a horrible mix of emotions he couldn't quite reconcile, Warrehn's hateful blue eyes still at the forefront of his mind.

"What are you two still doing here?"

Samir flinched so badly he nearly fell off his chair. He lifted his gaze and found Warrehn in the doorway, surveying them with narrowed eyes.

"I beg your pardon?" Dalatteya said, stiffening in her seat.

"I told you to get out of my house."

Swallowing, Samir glanced around the room. "Could you leave us, please?" he said, addressing the servants.

They bowed to him and left, not even glancing at Warrehn. The latter watched the exchange with a dark look, his telepathic presence like a thundercloud.

"You're making a mistake," Samir said quietly,

studying his own fingers before looking back at Warrehn. Holding his heavy gaze was difficult, but he refused to look away. "Servants talk. If you throw us out, it will look very bad for you. No one knows what to make of you. No one trusts you after you've been gone for nearly two decades. The fact that you're consorting with the rebels the majority of the population massively distrusts doesn't help, either. You'll have a rebellion on your hands if you keep it up."

"I'm the rightful king of this clan."

Samir nodded. "You are." Ignoring the furious hiss his mother let out, he said, looking at Warrehn, "But your bloodline doesn't entitle you to people's respect and love. For our people, my mother and I are the royals who led our country to prosperity. You're the royal who associates with the rebels and has been shirking his responsibilities for twenty years."

A muscle started working in Warrehn's jaw. If looks could kill, Samir would probably be dead now. Warrehn said, "That's not how it was."

"But that's how people see it," Dalatteya cut in, her voice cold as ice. "Besides, your father was a ruthless, uncaring king and people wouldn't want to have his son on the throne when they can have a monarch they love. *My* son is beloved by his people. He's kind, he's capable, and he's trustworthy. You are not." She sneered, looking at Warrehn like he was a bug under her shoe. "At least your father was intelligent. He was smart enough not to show what a major piece of shit he was. People didn't know how bad Emyr really was. He fooled a lot of people with his looks and smiles before he stabbed them in the back."

"Just like you, huh?" Warrehn said.

Dalatteya paled. Her lips barely moving, she bit out, "I'm nothing like him. Nothing."

Warrehn leaned a wide shoulder against the doorway and raised his eyebrows mockingly. "I see no difference. Wait, no, I know one: my father didn't target children. He was a better person than you could ever hope to be."

Dalatteya sprang to her feet, her eyes gleaming with an odd fire. "You know nothing, you foolish boy! You didn't know him as *I* did. Emyr was the worst man I've ever known—heartless, selfish, cruel, arrogant—"

"He was my father," Warrehn stated in a flat voice. "He wasn't perfect, but he was far from being a monster. His biggest flaw was his unhealthy fixation on you."

Dalatteya went still.

Warrehn smiled grimly. "What, you thought I didn't know? I was ten, not a small child. Everyone knew where he spent the nights, including my mother and your husband. My mother always said you bewitched him and that you'd be the death of him one day. At the time, I thought she was just jealous, but she was right, wasn't she? My father is dead because he put his dick into a viper and kept going back."

He glanced at Samir and sneered at them both. "Frankly, I don't get the appeal, and it has nothing to do with me preferring men. Your son is your carbon copy, and I've seen ten-credit whores more appealing than the present company."

Samir flushed, half-incredulous, half-offended.

Dalatteya stared at Warrehn for a long moment before smiling. It was a very nice smile. A dangerous smile.

She rounded the table, her heels clicking on the floor as she moved gracefully toward Samir. Laying a delicate hand on Samir's arm, she pulled him to his feet and pushed him toward Warrehn.

"It always amuses me how simple men are," she said as Warrehn watched them approach with a wary, distrustful expression. Dalatteya's gaze moved to Samir and their familial bond flared with, *Trust me.*

Confused but curious to see what his mother had planned, Samir nodded.

Dalatteya looked back at Warrehn. "I don't know if you remember, but Emyr was always terrible at listening to his advisers. He was too headstrong and arrogant to care for anyone's opinion besides his own. But he was always ever so agreeable after—how did you put it? Ah, yes: after 'putting his dick into a viper.' I did wonder if you inherited his weakness. From the way you keep glancing at my son, it seems you have."

What are you doing, Mother? Samir pushed at her through their bond, but Dalatteya ignored him, smiling as Warrehn's glare intensified.

"He's beautiful, isn't he?" Dalatteya said, pushing Samir in front of Warrehn and forcing Warrehn to look at him—and scowl deeper. "So *lovely.* That's what your father called me as he forced himself on me. He is lovely, don't you think?"

"Shut your mouth," Warrehn gritted out, looking away from Samir and scowling at Dalatteya. "Are you seriously trying to whore your son out to me? I didn't think I could think worse of you, but you've just proven me wrong."

Dalatteya's smile widened. "Oh, I have no intention of ever letting you lay as much as a finger on my son. It was bad enough that I had to endure your father's attentions. No son of his would ever touch mine. I'm simply proving that you can't claim the moral high ground when you're very much your father's son."

Warrehn chuckled. "It's hilarious—and fucked-up—that you think superficial lust is a bigger crime than the murder of an entire family, including kids, and regicide. You're fucking insane—and beyond obsessed with a dead man. My father is *dead*."

Dalatteya's face went unnaturally blank.

Samir looked at his mother curiously, once again wondering about her relationship with Emyr. Her feelings for him seemed far more complex than simple hatred.

Samir cleared his throat. "If you two are quite done talking about me like I'm not in the room, I'd like to eat," he said, before looking at Warrehn. "Prove to my mother that you aren't your father and actually listen to some sensible, honest advice: you can't afford to kick us out of the palace. That would be terrible optics. But if you're so determined to be a stubborn prick, be my guest. You're only playing into my mother's hands."

Warrehn stared at him, his expression searching. Intent.

Samir got the oddest feeling in his head and it took him a moment to realize what the sensation was: Warrehn was reading his mind. It was a subtle sensation, but not subtle enough.

"Done snooping?" Samir said. "Now get out of my head."

Warrehn didn't even have the decency to look ashamed. If anything, his gaze became sharp with curiosity. "Your telepathy isn't bound," he said. "Your childhood bond is broken, nearly non-existent. Why?"

Samir felt his mother tense up. She sent him a warning look, but Samir didn't need it. He was hardly going to spill his most shameful secret to a man who would use it against him.

"My bondmate is dead," he said. "Not that it's any of your concern. If you try snooping in my head again, I will report you. It is a crime, and one that wouldn't look good in your situation in particular."

The impossible man didn't look concerned in the least. The sharp curiosity was still burning in Warrehn's eyes, and Samir struggled to keep a composed look on his face. Something about this man's intensity was highly unsettling, making him feel off-balance—more off-balance than he had already felt.

"So should we pack our things or not?" Samir said, breaking the silence.

Warrehn looked at him some more. Then he pulled out his communicator and walked away, speaking on it quietly.

Samir stared after him in frustration. Was that a no or a yes?

"He wants you," Dalatteya said.

Samir flinched and tore his gaze away from Warrehn's back. "Don't be silly, Mother. You heard him."

Dalatteya's plush lips folded into a sneer. "Trust me, I know what I'm talking about. He can deny it all he wants, but he keeps looking at you unnecessarily—and he stares. He tries to mask it with scowls, but I know men. He's attracted to you, even if it's a superficial attraction based on just physical appearance." Her expression became thoughtful. "We could use it, perhaps."

Samir sighed and wondered idly why he couldn't have been born to a simple woman who didn't scheme as she breathed. "I thought you 'wouldn't let him lay a finger' on me?"

"And I won't. No son of Emyr will touch mine. But we could use his attraction in several ways. Come."

Taking his arm, she led him to the terrace outside. They walked deeper into the gardens before she spoke again. "It's not a secret that Warrehn isn't bonded. His childhood bond to his betrothed was entirely dissolved recently, so he's very free to form attachments and pursue his desires. His unbonded state is an additional source of distrust toward him. The prevalent opinion among the population is that his unbonded state indicates that he's too aggressive and less in control of his actions. We could use that. We could use his reluctant attraction to you to accuse him of sexual assault if you two were caught in an ambiguous situation. That would completely push public opinion in our favor and would potentially result in a civil uprising—and revolution."

"No," Samir said, grimacing. "I don't want to unnecessarily spill blood and hurt our economy."

"*Unnecessarily?*"

Samir sighed.

"Yes. I can't use our people that way. Civil war isn't what I've been working for all these years."

"Don't be foolish. Do you really think that brute is capable of ruling our grand clan and would lead it to prosperity?"

"I don't know," he said honestly. "We hardly know him. But he was ten when his parents died. Surely the former king had started teaching him already before his death?"

Dalatteya made a derisive sound. "Emyr wasn't very involved in his sons' upbringing. Between ruling the country and making my life hell, he didn't have time for anything else."

"Still," Samir said. "He likely picked up something from Lord Tai'Lehr if he was raised in his house."

"It doesn't signify," she said dismissively. "A good monarch should always be prepared to make some necessary sacrifices for the greater good of the country. Civil war would have collateral damage, but it's necessary in this case."

"No."

"Darling," his mother said in a chillingly gentle voice. "You do realize that if you're against this, the only other option is to remove Warrehn from the picture?"

Samir almost laughed. He envied his mother's ability to talk about killing someone in such nonchalant terms.

"I refuse to believe that killing a person is the only option," he said firmly.

Dalatteya sighed. They walked in silence for a while.

"There's another option, I suppose," she said at last. "You could use his attraction to you to make him abdicate."

Samir did laugh this time. "Please—it's never going to happen. No one would give up their kingdom for the sake of lust, Mother."

Giving him a flat look, Dalatteya said, "Do I need to hire another history teacher for you? How many wars have been fought because of men's lust? The Great War was one, among others."

Samir flushed. His mother did have a point. "Fine, you're right. But I'm not convinced that he wants me at all."

"Trust me, he does. I know men. I know men of that family in particular. His attraction to you might be superficial, but nothing stirs a man's cock as much as the desire to have something he's told he can't have. Admit it, I'm right."

"Mother," Samir said with a pinched look, torn between laughing and being scandalized.

But when he looked at Dalatteya's face, all his amusement was gone. Her expression was strange: faraway and unamused, her blue eyes dark with an emotion he couldn't read.

"He only got more lustful when I told him that he couldn't have me," she said, almost absently. "The more I said no, the more it inflamed his desire. Men of that family are unhealthily obsessive, Samir. If Warrehn is anything like his father, the fact that I told him that he can't have you will only make him more attracted to you."

Samir looked at her carefully, hesitating. "Mother… May I ask you something? About your relationship with the late king?"

Dalatteya tensed up but nodded stiffly after a moment.

"Why didn't you follow your plan yourself? Expose him as an assaulter—as a rapist? Not even a king is above the law."

His mother looked away, her beautiful profile betraying no emotion. She stopped in front of a gorgeous violet flower and touched its petals with her graceful, delicate fingers. "Emyr had these planted because of me, you know. He said some nonsense about them matching my hair." Her lips pursed tightly. "I should have burned them years ago."

Samir stared at her, disturbed by her refusal—or inability—to give a straight answer. "You hated him, right?"

"Of course I did." Her throat moved. "I still do. I just… He was the thing poisoning my life and my thoughts for decades. He was the first thing I thought about in the morning for years and it's hard to train myself out of the habit. He's gone. I'm free. I'm happy. Thrilled."

She tore a petal off the flower, and then another, before crushing them in her fist. "I will not allow *his* son to ruin the life I've built for myself. I won't. That would mean he won. I can't allow that."

Fuck. Warrehn was right: his mother really was obsessed with a dead man.

Samir looked away, deeply uncomfortable and unsure what to think. King Emyr had been dead for two decades, for heaven's sake. Why couldn't his mother move on?

"Regardless," Dalatteya said suddenly, with a nonchalance that seemed a little too studied to be natural. "Let's return to the subject at hand. If Warrehn is anything like his father, his lustful, obsessive nature will be his weakness. Make him obsessed with you and talk him into abdicating—or I'll be taking other measures. Frankly, I prefer the latter option, but if you're so squeamish, fine, I shall give you some time to resolve the issue another way."

Samir nearly laughed. That was a choice between a very bad option and a terrible one. His mother was impossible.

But he knew she was dead serious. She wouldn't allow Emyr's son to take away what she saw as hers. It wasn't about Samir or even Warrehn; it was his mother's vendetta against a dead man. A dead man she clearly had very complex feelings for.

"I thought you didn't want him to lay a finger on me," Samir said dryly.

"I don't," Dalatteya said, grimacing. "But you don't have to do much with him to accomplish the goal. He's lonely, all by himself in a hostile place. It shouldn't be too difficult to make him fixate on you if you play your cards right, with the way he looks at you already."

Sighing, Samir rubbed the bridge of his nose. "I still think you're vastly overestimating my appeal."

His mother gave him an unimpressed look. "Don't be ridiculous. The only man on the planet who can rival you in appearance is Prince Jamil—and perhaps his younger brother. Warrehn would have to be dead not to find you appealing. Think about it."

And with that, she left.

Chapter 4

Turned out it was difficult to seduce someone who was actively avoiding you. Or at least it felt like Warrehn was avoiding him. Over the next week, Samir barely saw Warrehn. When Warrehn wasn't accepting calls from politicians and his lord-vassals, he was busy running the country, having relieved Samir and Dalatteya of their duties.

His mother was incensed, of course. More worryingly, she'd taken to disappearing for hours without informing Samir of what she was doing—and what she was planning.

It made Samir anxious. He was genuinely starting to get worried that his mother was plotting Warrehn's death. She'd even stopped asking about his progress on the seduction front, which wasn't encouraging at all.

Not that Samir was all that eager to report on his progress—or lack thereof.

It wasn't that Samir was prudish. Nor was he a virgin. Since he didn't have a bondmate and his sex drive was fully functional, he'd had sex. Sometimes. Very rarely—when he had time to discreetly visit certain high-profile establishments on pleasure planets. So yes, he liked sex just fine, his weird sexual preferences notwithstanding.

Anyway.

He liked sex just fine. The problem was, he'd never set out to seduce someone, especially for such a cold, pragmatic reason. It made him uncomfortable, like he was the villain of some over-the-top GlobalNet drama.

The thought made Samir chuckle. By most people's standards, he and his mother *were* the villains. If he followed through with the seduction plan, he would be. But he had no choice. His mother would simply finish what she'd started years ago if Samir did nothing: she clearly couldn't be reasonable about King Emyr's son.

He needed to act, and fast. He didn't trust his mother not to do something rash soon, since Warrehn's coronation was fast approaching.

Finally, Samir had gotten lucky: Warrehn seemed to be alone that evening. None of his hangers-on were present, and the palace AI informed Samir that the crown prince was in his office alone, having asked not to be disturbed.

It was his chance.

Taking a deep breath, Samir was about to enter Warrehn's office when the sound of Warrehn's voice through a crack in the door stopped him.

"—it's driving me crazy, Rohan." Warrehn's low voice was tight with frustration. "They're all two-faced snakes who smile at me as they think about how to use me. But I have to pretend not to notice a thing and play their inane games."

"That's politics for you, War," another voice said, likely through a communicator, since Warrehn was supposedly alone. "You'll have to get used to it."

"I know," Warrehn said, but he sounded utterly fed up.

There was some silence.

"How are things with the family?"

Warrehn let out a rough-sounding laugh. "You mean the viper and her spawn? They're still here. Which obviously doesn't help. I hate that I can't relax even in my own home. It doesn't feel like my own home sometimes with the servants being so loyal to the perfect Prince Samir and his perfect mother, even the droids. I heard a robot maid yesterday bemoaning the unfairness of me taking away 'Prince Samir's throne.' I feel like a fucking usurper." Warrehn laughed again. It lacked any mirth.

"He and his mother are very popular, War," Rohan said. "I warned you about it. You need to be careful about how you deal with them. I've been monitoring your grand clan's social media when I have time, and people don't seem convinced that you're the rightful king, regardless of your bloodline. With the way things are, Dalatteya could have you assassinated and people wouldn't mind even if the foul play is obvious."

Warrehn sighed.

"What are you suggesting I do?"

"Considering your distaste for politics and lying, your options are limited," Rohan said. "You could marry a popular noble from your clan. You could actually try to smile once in a while."

"Fuck off."

"I'm serious, War. Your blood isn't enough. People must actually like you to want you on the throne. You shouldn't make things easier for Dalatteya and her son by being an antisocial prick no one likes."

"I don't give a fuck about being liked," Warrehn said flatly. "What I want is to get them out of my house without backlash. They're plotting something, I'm sure of it. I'm surprised they haven't attempted to poison me yet, though maybe they know that I have a robot scanning all my food."

Samir's eyebrows flew up. Really? Talk about paranoia. Then again, it was probably justified, given his mother's plans.

"They're likely biding their time," Rohan said. "I agree that they are unlikely to give up without a fight. Why don't you read their thoughts to find out what they're planning? You're one of the most powerful telepaths on the planet. It should be easy for you."

Samir tensed up and waited for Warrehn's answer with bated breath.

"I tried," Warrehn said, a hint of frustration entering his voice. "But the mental traps in her mind don't let me go deeper beyond her surface thoughts. They must have become more aggressive and vigilant since you nearly sprang one. Whoever placed them had a hell of a skill. Some of her memories have clearly been tampered with and some are false to fool the intruder, but I can't retrieve the originals without springing the traps."

Samir tensed up. His mother had mental traps in her mind? Her memories had been tampered with? By whom? Why?

"What about the prince?" Rohan said, snapping him out of his thoughts.

When Warrehn didn't reply immediately, his friend said, "Warrehn?"

"I don't want to touch his mind."

Samir frowned.

"Why?" Rohan said, sounding puzzled.

It took Warrehn a moment to reply. "His mind is compatible with mine," he said stiffly. "I don't want my judgment to be influenced by that. The less I touch his mind, the better."

Samir blinked, unsure what to think or feel.

Considering that most people he knew were bonded, he'd rarely had an opportunity to touch someone else's mind intimately, so he wasn't sure what Warrehn meant.

"I have to go," Warrehn said suddenly. "I'll call you tomorrow."

Samir wondered if Rohan was as confused as he was by the sudden end of the conversation, but before he could give it much thought, the door was yanked open and he found himself staring at Warrehn's hard face.

"Learn anything?" he said, raising his finely shaped thick eyebrows.

Samir was too worried to feel embarrassed. "What is it about my mother's mind you were talking about? You said her memories have been tampered with and that there are traps in her mind."

Warrehn crossed his arms over his chest and stared him down, his face like stone. Samir tried not to feel intimidated, but it was so difficult. Everything about this man gave off strength and power that was both intangible and physical. Samir was in great shape himself, pretty well-built and tall, but next to Warrehn he felt small and insignificant. It was almost obscene, the way Warrehn's black shirt stretched over his biceps, broad shoulders, and muscular chest. Warrehn's sheer *presence* was overwhelmingly strong, too. He exuded the kind of power that was difficult to put into words. Samir could easily believe that he was one of the most powerful telepaths on the planet, as Rohan had said.

"Why should I tell you anything?" Warrehn said, looking at him impassively. "Your mother literally wants me dead."

Samir winced on the inside. He did have a point. "I don't," he said.

Warrehn's brows drew together. "What?"

"I don't want you dead," Samir said, looking him in the eyes with his most earnest expression.

For a moment, Warrehn seemed to be almost softening before his face hardened again. He scoffed, giving him a look of disgust. "I don't trust a word you say. You're as slimy as your mother. Get out."

"I'd just like to talk to you," Samir said with a smile. "We didn't really have any opportunity to catch up, and I thought—"

"Don't waste your breath. You can go back to your viper of a mother and tell her that I'm not interested in repeating my father's mistakes."

Samir stared at him—or rather, at his rich honey-brown hair, since Warrehn had turned his back to him. The hair in question looked amazingly thick and soft, gleaming in the light. It seemed completely unsuitable for this hard, unyielding man. "Pardon? What is that supposed to mean?"

Warrehn let out a humorless laugh. "I know what you're up to. I'm not an idiot. So get out. I'm not interested. I'm not my father—I don't think with my cock."

"Your father didn't think with his cock," Samir said, just to be contrary, even though he was sure of no such thing. "He had feelings for my mother, even if they were messed up."

Warrehn looked back at him, his lips twisted into something that wasn't a smile. "Yes, I know he 'loved' her. And look where it got him. Love is a disease that turns even the smartest men into fools. I'm no fool. Now stop wasting my time."

Samir cocked his head to the side, eyeing him thoughtfully.

He suddenly wondered how bad it would have been to grow up with a neglectful father who was only interested in chasing after a woman—a woman who wasn't Warrehn's mother. No wonder Warrehn sneered at the mere notion of love.

Samir opened his mouth, but closed it as he realized that it was pointless. This man was determined to hate him, and nothing he could say would change that.

He turned and left, feeling defeated and out of sorts.

Chapter 5

Warrehn's coronation took place two days later.

It was a very public ceremony neither Samir nor his mother was invited to participate in.

His mother was angry at the public slight—but also gleeful, because their absence during the coronation made displeasure with Warrehn grow among the common folk and the court. The slight looked particularly bad, considering that Dalatteya had hosted a ball in Warrehn's honor and had been nothing but courteous and kind in public. It made Warrehn look like a royal ass.

"He must be the least popular king our grand clan has ever seen," Dalatteya said, setting her multi-device down and smiling. "Have you seen his ratings? There are already protests all over the country. He's one misstep away from an open revolt."

Samir wasn't as happy about the prospect as his mother was. A civil war wasn't something he'd ever wanted for his grand clan. It would lead to bloodshed and sanctions from the other grand clans, and that would destroy their economy.

"Don't look at me that way," Dalatteya said, raising her eyebrows. "It's his own fault. For once, I did nothing. Well, almost nothing, besides a few strategically dropped comments around certain lord-vassals."

"Mother," Samir said exasperatedly.

"It's not my fault he's too stubborn to play politics. The current state of affairs is entirely his own doing." She looked very pleased. "I didn't expect it to be so easy. Emyr was never as shortsighted as his son. We won't even have to do anything. All we need to do now is wait."

Samir just shook his head, but it wasn't like his mother was wrong. Warrehn's shaky political standing was mostly his own doing. On the bright side, he wouldn't have to seduce Warrehn if things worked out as his mother expected them to.

Now the waiting game began.

***

They would never know if Warrehn's political standing would have deteriorated enough to lead to an open revolt, because a few days later, Warrehn brought home his younger brother, who had turned out to be alive.

And that changed everything.

Apparently, Prince Eruadarhd—or Eridan, as he called himself now—wasn't actually killed in the attack all those years ago. And he was now Warrehn's heir if something were to happen to Warrehn.

It probably went without saying that Samir's mother was furious. Now taking Warrehn out of the picture wouldn't accomplish anything. Moreover, Eridan looked uncannily like the late queen-consort, who had been beloved by the common folk, and their people seemed to be softening toward Warrehn by proxy. The revolt that had seemed all but inevitable a few days ago was now just a distant possibility.

Everyone was too busy discussing the miraculous return of the long-lost, beautiful prince who had been raised by the monks of the High Hronthar, and the happy reunion between the brothers. It was the good press Warrehn had so badly needed, so Eridan's return completely ruined Dalatteya's plans.

And yet, Samir's mother seemed rather fond of Eridan—which made no sense.

"Something is amiss," she said, rubbing at her temples with a frustrated look on her face. "I *like* Eridan. I should despise him as much as I despise Emyr's other spawn. And yet, I like him. It's inexplicable."

Frowning, Samir sat up straighter. "You think someone has messed with your mind?"

His mother's lips thinned. She said nothing, but her silence was answer enough: she clearly had similar suspicions.

"Who?" Samir said. "Do you think it has something to do with the mind traps in your mind that Warrehn mentioned?"

"I think…" she said, looking away. "I think it's the High Hronthar. The mind adepts aren't as harmless and apolitical as they pretend to be."

"What?" Samir stared at her. "What makes you think so?"

Dalatteya's expression became blank. "Emyr has told me. He told me to never stay alone with them or look them in the eye if I could help it."

Suppressing the urge to tell her that it was bizarre of her to trust the words of a man she had hated—and had killed—Samir considered it for a moment. "But why? Why would someone from the High Hronthar mess with your mind to make you like Eridan?"

"That is the question, isn't it," Dalatteya murmured, her face pensive. "The latest revelation that they have been hiding Eridan all these years almost certainly proves that they have their own agenda. I wouldn't be surprised if they groomed Eridan into their puppet with the intention to place him on the throne when the time was right."

Samir still had trouble believing that. But he supposed that would explain why the mind adepts of the High Hronthar would mess with his mother's mind. Dalatteya wasn't even sure why she had been so confident that Eridan was dead when the body had never been found. That conviction—as well as her positive disposition toward Eridan—could have been planted in her mind. It wasn't impossible.

Either way, the result was the same: with Eridan's return, there was no longer a point in trying to remove Warrehn from the throne.

Truth be told, Samir was relieved. All the options they'd had—seduction, revolution, or assassination—ranged from bad to horrible. He did want to be the king, yes, but he wanted to be a decent person more. Maybe he really was *soft*, as his mother said, but Samir was fine with it.

So he gave Warrehn and his brother a wide berth, relieved not to have to deal with Warrehn's hard, disdainful gaze on him.

Not that Warrehn didn't look at him at all. Samir still caught him looking at him sometimes—before quickly looking away.

It made him wonder.

Samir also wondered why Warrehn seemed to look unhappier and more stressed as the days turned into months.

He often saw Warrehn lurking in the darkest corners of the ballrooms, clearly not wanting the attention his status as a king warranted. Eridan seemed to be the one doing most of the socializing, but Samir noticed that even Eridan's bright smiles started to turn strained with every passing day.

That was why Samir wasn't very surprised when one morning he woke up to the news of Eridan leaving the palace and returning to the monastery.

Calluvian Society Gossip
PRINCE ERIDAN: I MISS MY HOME

In an unexpected turn of events, Prince Eridan of the Fifth Grand Clan doesn't wish to be a prince. Raised by the mind adepts of the High Hronthar, the prince reportedly feels more at home at the austere monastery than he does at the lavish palace of his brother.

"I love Warrehn very much, and I'm ever so grateful that we have found each other again," Prince Eridan said. "But the Order has been my home since I was three years old, and I'm so grateful to my brother for allowing me to return to the life I'm used to. My greatest ambition is to become a certified mind adept of the Order, but it doesn't mean I will stop being Warrehn's brother. I support him in everything."

Samir closed the article and thought of the ramifications of it.

One thing was for sure: his mother was going to be thrilled.

Chapter 6

Samir stood beside his mother on the grand staircase of the palace as they watched Warrehn say his goodbyes to Eridan. The brothers hugged, Eridan's slim form almost comically tiny in the king's arms.

"What a turn of events," Dalatteya said quietly, her tone thoughtful.

Samir made a noncommittal noise, watching the brothers part. Warrehn's face was like stone despite the tight hug he'd given his brother.

"Look at him," Dalatteya murmured. "He feels so angry. Lost. Lonely. His brother has abandoned him. He's so alone. Now is the perfect time to act, my dear."

Samir looked at Warrehn's tense, hunched shoulders and nodded in agreement. Warrehn did seem angry and lonely, even though he was clearly trying not to show it for Eridan's sake.

"What are you suggesting, Mother?" Samir said, suppressing a sigh. It appeared that now that Eridan was out of the picture, the plotting against Warrehn was on.

"Provoking a public uprising isn't possible right now," his mother said, drumming a manicured finger over the railing. "Eridan has garnered quite a bit of public sympathy for his brother in the past few months. Unless Warrehn makes a huge misstep, that sympathy won't evaporate overnight. So there are only two options: either Warrehn abdicates willingly or he'll have to be removed."

Samir nearly laughed at the casual way his mother was discussing murder and regicide. The worst part was, he couldn't even tell her that he'd take no part in this: if he did, she would just have Warrehn *removed*, Samir's opinion be damned. This way he could at least know what she was planning.

"I don't think I can seduce him," Samir said. "He saw right through me the last time I tried."

"It's all right, darling," she said, still watching Warrehn. "It doesn't matter. I may have found another solution."

Samir narrowed his eyes. "Mother, what are you planning?"

Dalatteya just smiled and started talking about the ball she was going to attend that night.

Sometimes his mother was absolutely infuriating.

***

Since Eridan's departure, Samir noticed that Warrehn had been avoiding social functions.

But the court day was obviously an exception. It didn't matter how much Warrehn might detest socializing; he was the king, and the court day was one of the social functions he wasn't allowed to avoid.

Warrehn also couldn't forbid Samir from attending without giving the gossipmongers a lot to talk about. Traditionally, the king had his heir next to him as he greeted his lord-vassals, and with Eridan gone, that role fell to Samir.

Warrehn certainly didn't look happy to have him there, judging by the stony expression on his face as Samir sat down in the seat to the left of his throne.

Not that he ever looks happy, Samir thought uncharitably, dragging his eyes away from the king, a little annoyed by how often his gaze seemed to gravitate toward a man who hadn't even deigned to give him more than a glance since Samir's arrival.

It wasn't as though he wanted Warrehn to look at him; Samir didn't exactly relish being the object of his disdainful gaze. It was just… It irked him that Warrehn had no trouble ignoring him when Samir couldn't do the same, hyperaware of the king's presence beside him. Warrehn was just so difficult to ignore. Maybe it was his size—the way his tall, powerful body occupied the throne, somehow both relaxed and tense. Samir could see Warrehn's hand on the armrest of the throne in his peripheral vision, and there was a fine tension in that hand, the veins standing in sharp relief despite Warrehn's seemingly relaxed posture. The signet ring on Warrehn's finger gleamed brightly, a stark contrast to his otherwise somber, dark attire.

His fingers were elegant despite their size, and well groomed, which somewhat surprised Samir. He had trouble imagining Warrehn giving a fuck about how his hands looked. Though the fact that he hadn't bothered to remove the dark hair on his knuckles was well in character.

Samir looked at his own professionally manicured, hairless fingers, pale and almost slim compared to Warrehn's, and wondered what they would look like against Warrehn's larger, bronzed hand.

He blinked at the bizarre thought and pushed it away, straightening in his chair and dragging his eyes from Warrehn's hand.

It was neither the time nor the place to entertain inane thoughts. He was seated next to the king and the court was watching them.

Thankfully, he was so used to the court days that greeting nobles and murmuring pleasantries was second nature to him; he could do it in his sleep.

Unlike him, Warrehn clearly felt out of his element. He still didn't know most of these people well, and his grim silence and abrupt manner didn't exactly endear him to anyone.

Samir suppressed a wince when Warrehn barely glanced at Lord Vahir when the man bowed to him. That was such a huge mistake. Lord Vahir was one of the most influential lord-vassals of their grand clan. He was a very proud, very vain man—he would consider Warrehn's dismissive attitude a deliberate slight.

Samir glanced at his mother at the other end of the courtroom and found her smiling a little as she waited for Lord Vahir's reaction. She didn't have to wait long.

"I wonder, Your Majesty," Lord Vahir said, his tone very polite. "How come Prince Eridan chose to return to the austere life of a monk over a life in this splendid palace with his only living relative? I'm sure you are not to blame, but it seems... *odd*. I wonder what made him so unhappy here."

Murmurs rolled through the room.

Samir barely kept his expression neutral. While he had expected some kind of retribution for the perceived slight, he hadn't expected that Vahir would dare to insinuate that there must have been something wrong with Eridan's relationship with the king for Eridan to leave so abruptly. It was very clever, Samir had to admit. Or foolish—if the way Warrehn's telepathic presence darkened with anger was any indication.

Samir shivered, glancing at Warrehn's stony face. Those hard blue eyes were now giving Vahir their full attention, and Vahir shifted a little, clearly somewhat nervous. Samir could relate: he could attest that being the object of that intensity was highly unsettling.

Everyone in the court seemed to be holding their breaths as they expected the king to react to the not-so-subtle insult. Knowing Warrehn's temper, Samir half-expected him to explode, but he looked surprisingly calm, his face betraying nothing.

When Warrehn spoke, his voice was hard and flat. "I imagine he left for the same reason your eldest son left your clan, Lord Vahir."

Vahir paled and then flushed as another wave of whispers rolled through the room. Vahir's heir had famously refused to come back to Calluvia after finishing his education on another planet. Only Vahir's immense influence had stopped his family from becoming the subject of ridicule and nasty gossip. Heirs to noble Calluvian families simply didn't leave their fortunes like that. Something had to be amiss. But no one spoke of that scandal anymore—Vahir had hushed it up well.

Samir was torn between laughing and facepalming. Warrehn's response was so unwise, so horrible politically, but it had sure put Vahir in his place and would teach him not to insult the king to his face.

Warrehn smiled at Vahir, a cold smile that was all teeth and didn't reach his eyes. "Just like your former heir, my brother has found another calling. Who are we to stop them from pursuing it?"

Vahir bowed.

"Indeed, Your Majesty," he ground out and then bowed again and left. Halfway to the door, Dalatteya approached Vahir and tucked her hand into his elbow. They left the room together, speaking quietly.

Suppressing a sigh, Samir murmured, just for Warrehn's ears, "That was very entertaining, but very unwise."

Warrehn shifted his heavy gaze to him for the first time that evening. "Is that a threat?"

Laughing a little, Samir shook his head. "No. I'm just stating the obvious. Your PR team is going to chew you out for this. Mine would for sure if I publicly humiliated one of the most influential lord-vassals of our clan."

Warrehn's brows drew together. He looked away, before looking back at Samir, and then averted his gaze again, his hand gripping the armrest of the throne. "I hate politics."

"I've noticed," Samir said wryly. "But you'll have to pay attention to the politics if you don't want your approval ratings to drop like a rock. Do you have any idea how much influence lords like Vahir have?"

"Why are you being so talkative and helpful all of a sudden?" Warrehn said, without looking at him. "If this is another attempt to seduce me with lovely smiles, don't waste your time. I'm not buying what you're selling."

Lovely smiles?

"I'm just making conversation," Samir said. "Or am I not allowed to talk to you, Your Majesty?"

Warrehn gave him a long, scrutinizing look that made something in Samir's stomach squirm.

He suppressed the urge to fidget and touch his hair, unsure why he felt so agitated.

Fuck, no other person had ever unsettled him as much as this man did.

"...Um, Your Majesty? Your Highness?"

Samir tore his gaze from Warrehn's sharp blue eyes and turned to the speaker, feeling a little disoriented.

He stared at the woman blankly for a moment before finally focusing on her face enough to recognize her.

He forced a smile and made some small talk with her, doing his best to ignore the silent man by his side.

It was impossible. He was so hyperaware of him that his attention strayed every time Warrehn as much as twitched a little in his peripheral vision. It was a good thing Samir could do small talk in his sleep.

After some time, he gave in and looked at Warrehn.

He found him looking at him, a deep frown on his face.

Samir gave him a questioning look.

You're good at it, said Warrehn's voice grudgingly in his head.

Samir froze, his eyes widening. It should have been impossible for Warrehn to send his thoughts into his mind. They didn't have any kind of telepathic bond. They weren't touching. Samir had his mental shields fully up. This should have been *impossible*. Just how powerful was Warrehn, exactly?

Samir bit his lip, disturbed and intrigued.

"Your Highness?"

Right. He was supposed to be talking to—what was her name, again?

"Next," Warrehn said flatly, barely glancing at the woman.

The woman flushed, pressed her lips together, and strode away after giving them a stiff bow.

"You should try being nice and polite once in a while, you know," Samir murmured as another noble started heading toward them.

Blue eyes shifted to him and looked for a moment, before looking away.

Samir was left staring at Warrehn's hard profile.

"I'm plenty nice, considering their thoughts," Warrehn said without looking at Samir.

"Reading someone's thoughts without permission definitely isn't *nice*. It is a crime—"

"As is murdering people."

"I didn't murder anyone."

"Being aware of a crime and helping the murderer to conceal it makes you complicit."

"I don't know what you're talking about," Samir said.

Warrehn looked back at him, his eyes flashing. "Sure you don't."

Samir glared at him, and Warrehn glared back, and Samir wanted to—he wanted to—

"Your Majesty. Your Highness."

Right.

Samir wrenched his gaze away from Warrehn and smiled blandly at the next person.

He couldn't hear a word they said.

Chapter 7

Warrehn'ngh'zaver would be the first to admit that he hated being wrong. No one liked being wrong, but it was particularly irritating that *Samir* had been right: his publicity team was less than impressed with him for his words to Lord Vahir.

"This is a disaster!" his press officer, Ayda, said, pacing Warrehn's office, looking at the datapad in her hands. "Your approval ratings have never been high, but they have reached a new low now that Lord Vahir has his people spreading the rumor that Prince Eridan left because of your unnatural inclinations."

Warrehn stiffened. "He did what?"

"He has people spreading the rumor that you wanted to bed your own brother and that's why Eridan ran off."

Warrehn closed his eyes and breathed, trying to control his rage.

"Don't kill him," Sirri cut in from the couch, studying her fingernails. "I know it's tempting, but that wouldn't help anything."

Warrehn looked at her in frustration. He wasn't sure what Sirri was even doing here. He certainly hadn't invited her. He'd never had an easy relationship with her. She was Rohan's distant cousin he'd basically grown up with. Sometimes Warrehn thought they were almost friends, except they never seemed to agree on anything.

"The sick fuck is spreading the rumor that I want to fuck Eri and I'm supposed to do nothing?" Warrehn bit off.

"Killing him would only make you look guiltier," Sirri pointed out.

"I can make it untraceable."

"You? You have about as much subtlety as a bull in a china shop. Leave it alone, War. Let the professionals handle it." She nodded toward Ayda.

Warrehn sighed and loosened his cravat, leaning back in his chair. "What are you suggesting, then?"

"We can't deny the rumor—acknowledging it would only make it worse," Ayda said. "You just need some good press. Some *really* good press to help your ratings."

"What kind of press?" Warrehn said, pinching the bridge of his nose. He was already getting a headache.

"You need to show up at various charity events with someone of impeccable reputation, someone well liked and popular among the court and common people—"

"No," Warrehn said, sensing where it was going.

"Prince Samir," Ayda finished, as if not hearing him. "He was an amazing ruler for this country during your absence. Your association with him would fix your approval ratings."

Warrehn frowned. "I thought the regent was the one ruling our clan."

Ayda said, "Not at all—at least not since the prince turned twenty. Her Excellency obviously had the seat on the Council of Twelve Grand Clans, but it's not a secret that Prince Samir was the one making decisions in the past four years. Lady Dalatteya is probably the better politician, but Prince Samir is absolutely the superior leader and strategist. They say his grasp of macroeconomics is unrivaled on the planet. Our grand clan has the highest happiness rate across the planet for a reason—and that reason is Prince Samir."

"You're on my team, not his," Warrehn said, irritably.

At least his press officer had the grace to flush. "I'm telling you this because you need to understand why it has to be Prince Samir with you on the tour."

"I said no," Warrehn said.

"Why not?" Sirri cut in. "Yesterday you sure looked like you got on well enough, judging by the way you kept gazing into his pretty blue eyes and equally pretty lips."

Warrehn didn't even need to look at her to know she was smirking, hoping to rile him up. He refused to give her the satisfaction.

"Samir and I don't get along," he said, ignoring Sirri and looking at Ayda. "He wouldn't want to help me improve my ratings. I'm sure his mother is in league with Vahir and has a hand in spreading those disgusting rumors. Samir wouldn't do anything to make her position less strong."

"Aren't you the king?" Sirri said. "*Make* him."

Warrehn went still, his heart beating faster as he imagined using his position and making Samir do whatever he wanted. His cock twitched, and he gritted his teeth, disgusted with himself. *No.* His father's downfall had probably started with similar thoughts.

"I agree," Ayda said. "You're the head of the royal family and technically you can order Prince Samir to accompany you on a publicity tour—"

"It's a publicity tour now? I thought it was just a few public appearances."

"Anything less than a publicity tour across the country wouldn't change much. The rural areas need a lot of convincing—they're Prince Samir's most devoted supporters because of how much he has improved their quality of life and infrastructure. If they see you together, being friendly, it will help you enormously. We'll make the tour into an event: the new king is traveling across the country to see with his own eyes how his people are doing and to learn their needs. You will travel in a land vehicle—"

"Are you serious?" Warrehn said with a snort. "Maybe we should make it even more Middle Ages and travel in a carriage pulled by zywerns."

Sirri snickered, but Ayda gave him a stern look. "It's traditional for royal visits to the countryside to be made using a land vehicle, Your Majesty. Surely you're aware how old-fashioned people in the rural areas are."

"Fine," Warrehn said with a sigh. It seemed there was no arguing with her. "When will the tour start?"

Ayda smiled.

Warrehn left the room half an hour later and headed to Samir's wing. He needed to inform Samir that he would be accompanying him on the tour. He didn't expect that conversation to go well, especially when he found Samir with his mother.

"His Majesty the King," the AI announced as he entered Samir's drawing room.

Samir got to his feet while Dalatteya remained seated on the couch.

Warrehn surveyed them, quashing the surge of hatred at the sight of Dalatteya. It was both easier and harder to look at Samir. He really was Dalatteya's male copy, down to his full lips and long eyelashes. His firm jaw and fit, masculine body were the biggest differentiators, but they weren't enough to make Warrehn forget who his mother was.

Not that it stopped his body from reacting to him. He wasn't dead.

"Your Majesty," Samir said, with a slight question in his tone.

Warrehn didn't miss the way Dalatteya pursed her lips. Clearly the form of address annoyed her. Good.

"You will accompany me on a publicity tour across the country," Warrehn said, looking at Samir. "We're leaving in two days and will be traveling for twenty-four days. Prepare accordingly."

He turned and left before either of them could voice an objection.

He would have to prepare mentally too. Nearly a month in close quarters with a man he detested but wouldn't mind sticking his cock into sounded like a special sort of hell.

Chapter 8

Samir listened to his mother's incensed rant for half an hour, before finally cutting her off with, "He's the king, Mother. I must do as he says. Being angry wouldn't change anything."

Dalatteya stopped pacing, her expression becoming distant and thoughtful. "You're right. Perhaps… Perhaps we could use this."

Narrowing his eyes, Samir said, "Mother? What are you talking about?"

But Dalatteya hummed and changed the subject.

It was extremely annoying, but she refused to tell him what she was planning, no matter how much he prodded her.

"It would be better if you don't know," Dalatteya said at last. "He's a strong telepath. He might read your mind."

And that was that.

Samir wasn't happy, but he had no choice but to relent and simply wait for her to act.

He didn't have to wait long.

Next morning, he was woken up early by his mother and urged to get a hearty breakfast *right now*.

"In the smaller breakfast room," Dalatteya added.

Shooting her suspicious looks, Samir got dressed and headed there. His mother didn't accompany him.

When he entered the room, he paused, finding Warrehn seated at the head of the table. He was wearing all black, as usual, his gleaming golden-brown hair the only remotely not-grim thing about him.

"Good morning," Samir said.

Warrehn paused with his teacup at his mouth before giving a clipped nod.

Licking his lips, Samir walked closer and sat down to Warrehn's right, trying to act nonchalant and not give away that his heart was pounding. He was just nervous about his mother's plan. She must have sent him here for a reason.

A serving droid rolled to him and started serving him. Samir ate automatically, feeling ridiculously self-conscious, the silence in the room making his stomach feel funny.

He darted a look at Warrehn's hard face. Warrehn looked up, and their eyes met.

Samir moistened his lips with his tongue again and cleared his throat a little. "So we're leaving tomorrow morning, right?"

"Yes," Warrehn said, watching him with an intense expression Samir couldn't quite read.

Why are you looking at me? Stop looking at me, I can't stand it.

Samir tried to gather his thoughts. "What do you expect from me during the publicity tour?"

Warrehn opened his mouth to answer but went still, his eyes narrowing and his shoulders tensing up. His nostrils flared and his gaze darted around the room.

Frowning, Samir looked around too, but he couldn't see anything. "What is it?"

"There is someone in the room."

Samir let out a laugh. "There's no one here but us."

Warrehn got to his feet, his brows furrowed as his sharp gaze continued to search the room.

Samir's heart started to beat faster. Could Warrehn be correct? Was this part of his mother's plan?

"Why do you think so?" he said.

"I can sense them," Warrehn said shortly, his hand coming to rest on the table beside Samir.

Samir stared at those strong, tanned fingers blankly as Warrehn's meaning finally registered. He could sense people's presence without trying? Just how powerful was Warrehn?

"The ventilation shaft," Warrehn said, taking a few steps to the right and looking up. "It's ajar. Someone was there, but I can't sense them anymore."

Samir frowned, confused. He didn't understand.

Tugging at his cravat absently, he got to his feet, too, and walked to stand next to Warrehn. He… He wanted to be closer to him.

Suddenly, Warrehn stiffened and turned to look at Samir. "Do you feel it, too?" he said, his voice strained. He was breathing unsteadily, his jaw tense, his pupils unnaturally dilated.

Samir swallowed, suddenly aware that his cock was hard.

This… this wasn't normal. He usually didn't go from zero to full mast in under a second, for no reason.

Warrehn cursed elaborately, his expression darkening. "Fariz, security and a doctor to the breakfast room," he barked out. "Tell them to wear bio-hazard gear until we know what we're dealing with."

"Right away, Your Majesty," the palace AI said.

"Is this your doing?" Warrehn said, looming over Samir.

His heart beating faster, Samir wet his dry lips and shook his head, and Warrehn blue eyes followed the movement of his tongue, transfixed. Hungry.

Shit. *What* was going on? Samir's body felt on fire, his skin oversensitive, his clothes too rough and too numerous. He wanted to be naked. He wanted skin against skin. He wanted this big, hard man on top of him, rutting against him, into him, taking him hard and fast and—

"Fuck," Warrehn bit out, practically jumping away from Samir and staggering back as far from him as possible, to the other end of the room.

Security guards in bio-hazard suits entered the room. "Your Majesty?" they said.

Warrehn took a deep breath, looking pained, and ground out, "Restrain Prince Samir and don't let us come near each other until the doctor is here. Ignore any other orders I might give you."

"Yes, Your Majesty," the guards said.

Samir took a few steps toward Warrehn, but the guards stopped him, firmly holding him in place.

Warrehn twitched toward him and turned away with a curse, propping himself against the wall, his muscles bulging as he breathed like he'd run a marathon.

Doctor Jihan entered the room. "What's wrong, Your Majesty?"

Warrehn turned his head, his gaze not quite focused. "We've been drugged with something," he said in a clipped voice. "Something invisible and scentless. It should probably be still in the air."

The doctor frowned and pulled out a medical scanner. His frown deepened and he muttered something under his breath before saying more loudly, "Please tell me your symptoms, Your Majesty."

Warrehn didn't answer, his glazed eyes fixed on Samir. As if in a daze, he took a few steps in his direction, and Samir keened eagerly, panting as he struggled to free himself from the restrictive hold those men had on him. Why were they holding him? Who were these people? Why were they not letting him go? He wanted his mate.

"Restrain them both," someone said. "Bring them to the medical wing and order a decontamination team into the room. I'll need samples of the air. And Lady Dalatteya will need to be informed."

And then Samir was being pulled somewhere and people were talking to him, but he didn't care.

He wanted. He *burned*.

Where was he?

***

Dalatteya'il'zaver didn't like it when things didn't go according to her plans.

She had been promised that the plan would be carried out without a hitch and her son wouldn't be affected. So much for that.

Uriel had *a lot* of explaining to do.

Dalatteya grimaced as she glanced at her son. Samir's eyes were glassy, his face flushed and his lips bitten red as he struggled to get up from the examination table he was restrained against. Warrehn was outright growling, trying to free himself from his restraints and get to Samir, acting little better than a mindless beast. Their conditions had deteriorated alarmingly fast.

This was all *wrong*. The drug shouldn't have affected Warrehn this visibly, and definitely not so soon after he had inhaled it. Something had gone wrong.

"His Majesty and His Highness were drugged with an alien gaseous substance X137-1276," Doctor Jihan said, frowning at his medical scanner.

Dalatteya frowned, too. That definitely wasn't the drug Uriel had been supposed to use.

"It's a very rare substance outlawed on all the planets of the Union," the doctor said. "It's made primarily from the secondary mating glands of the primates from Planet Shoma. Those primates are near extinction and hunting them is forbidden—"

"I don't care what it's made from," Dalatteya snapped. "I want to know how anyone managed to infiltrate the palace!" Of course she knew perfectly well how that had been done, but she had to keep up appearances even here, in her own palace. There were ears everywhere. Although she preferred employing droids, unfortunately, medical droids weren't as good as real medical personnel. What she really wanted to know was how Uriel had ended up using the wrong drug—and drugging her son too. While Samir had been asleep, she had personally administered the antidote to the drug Uriel had been supposed to use. The drug shouldn't have affected him at all.

"That's not my area of expertise, my lady," the doctor said. "I can only give you my personal opinion. Historically, this drug was often used to incapacitate high-ranking political figures. While under its influence, a person cannot focus on anything but the object of his fixation. I suppose someone wanted the king to be unable to fulfill his duties."

That was a good potential motive she could use if the incident ever became known to the public. Warrehn hadn't exactly made many friends.

Any disgruntled noble could be blamed for this mess. The fact that her own son was affected too would divert the suspicion from her. That was a silver lining, she supposed.

"You still haven't told me in clear terms what the drug does."

Doctor Jihan was one of the best medical minds of the planet, but he blushed like a little boy at her question. "It... It makes the target fall into a dazed state of obsessive, uncontrollable lust for the person they had been with when they were dosed with the substance." He glanced at Samir. "Unfortunately, that was His Highness."

Samir didn't even seem to hear him, his gaze fixated longingly on Emyr's spawn, who was looking back at him just as transfixed, Warrehn's muscles flexing against the restraints, his nostrils flaring like that of a beast. It was utterly disgusting.

"... Prince Samir was dosed too, but the concentration of the substance is a little lower in his blood—it seems Prince Warrehn was the one closer to the ventilation shaft that was used to poison the air. Your son should be slightly more lucid and aware."

"He doesn't seem lucid at all," Dalatteya said, beyond frustrated. This was all wrong. The drug she had chosen was a slow-acting one. If everything had gone according to her plan, Warrehn wouldn't have even known that he had been drugged. He and Samir would have departed for the publicity tour utterly oblivious that Warrehn was a ticking bomb that was supposed to go off at a very precise time—the time Dalatteya would have arranged for someone to walk in on them as Warrehn attempted to force his lustful attentions on the unwilling Samir.

An attempted sexual assault on a member of royalty

was the sort of offense even a king wouldn't recover from, especially one who was so unpopular and who was already suspected of similar inclinations toward his younger brother—the rumor Dalatteya had carefully cultivated. If everything had come to pass, Warrehn would have been declared unfit to rule and removed from the throne by the decision of the Council. It had been such a simple plan—in theory.

Having her son compromised too hadn't been part of the plan. As Emyr would say, she had fucked up. The thought was extremely aggravating.

"If you pay attention, you will notice that he seems slightly aware of us while King Warrehn is completely transfixed by him." The doctor frowned at his medical scanner. "Right now the king is producing so many hormones I'm frankly amazed he hasn't passed out. His blood pressure is extremely concerning, despite the stabilizers he's on. It's quite literally life-threatening, as it can restrict blood flow to the heart, which may eventually lead to a heart attack."

Dalatteya didn't have to fake the look of concern. "What about my son?"

"His vitals are a little better, but…" The doctor sighed. "I'll be honest with you, my lady: his condition will deteriorate very soon too if we keep him restrained like this. I have tried suppressing the drug with various suppressors, but it's so alien that our medicine simply doesn't work on it. Sedatives don't work, either—their bodies are burning through them at an alarming rate, and using stronger sedatives is dangerous when we don't know how they would react with the alien drug in their systems. It might do more harm than good, and with how strained their vitals already are, I wouldn't recommend it."

Dalatteya swallowed. How? How could Uriel have made this mistake? He was normally so reliable and competent. Uriel was smarter than that. Even if the plan was carried out perfectly and Samir hadn't been affected, this drug's effects would have still been too obvious and Warrehn could rightly argue that he wasn't responsible for his actions under its influence. This was a disaster.

"Is there a cure?" Dalatteya said, unsure what answer she wanted to hear. She didn't want her son to be under the influence of that drug a moment longer. But if Warrehn was cured too, it would all be for nothing and they would be unlikely to get another opportunity to drug him. Warrehn would be extra vigilant from now on.

The doctor grimaced. "In a manner of speaking. His Majesty and His Highness must allow the drug to run its course and do what they must."

Dalatteya stared at him. "I beg your pardon?"

"They will have to indulge their impulses until the urge to… to fornicate passes."

"That is—that's preposterous! My son would never—" She cut herself off, glancing at her son's glassy, hungry gaze on Warrehn. She sighed. "You can't seriously expect me to believe that they absolutely need to—to indulge their base urges for the substance to wear off."

The doctor sighed. "That seems to be the only solution, my lady. I can't perform miracles in such a short time. The substance simulates the mating behavior of the primates that enter a frenzied mating season as soon as they imprint. Usually, the mating season of those primates ends with a successful pregnancy, which obviously isn't possible here, but Calluvian physiology is different enough for the drug to work a little differently. At least that's my hope."

"Hope?" Dalatteya repeated incredulously.

The doctor flushed. "I'm very sorry, my lady, but it's very hard to predict how our physiology would react to an alien substance. There is no documented case of Calluvians ever being drugged with that drug. It's all guesswork based on rumors and the experiences of the species that have similar biology to ours. But similar isn't the same."

At that moment, Samir strained against his restraints hard, keening pitifully when they didn't give. Warrehn growled in response, yanking at his own restraints. Hungry blue eyes with blown pupils were watching Samir's every move. Samir was returning the look, licking his lips and staring greedily at the very obvious bulge in Warrehn's pants.

It was utterly revolting.

"I think it'd be best if we leave them alone, my lady. My scanners detect a worrying jump in their blood pressure—"

"You can't be serious," Dalatteya said sharply.

"My lady, I understand that you're upset, but I'm afraid we have no other choice. Everything I know about such cases indicates that it's dangerous for their lives to leave them unfulfilled for long. Their vitals are alarming already."

Dalatteya glared at the doctor.

Rationally, she understood that he might be correct—but everything in her rebelled at the idea of allowing Emyr's spawn to put his hands on her son.

Samir made another desperate sound, tears of frustration falling down his cheeks as he unsuccessfully surged toward Warrehn again.

Dalatteya pursed her lips, torn.

She wouldn't give in.

She couldn't. But she hated seeing her son suffer. Absolutely couldn't stand it. And she wouldn't allow Emyr's spawn—*Emyr*—to be the reason her son got hurt.

"Fine," she said tersely and strode out of the room. If she didn't see it, she could pretend it wasn't happening.

And that it wasn't her fault.

Chapter 9

Samir was on fire—at least it felt like it. He felt overheated, too big for his own skin. He wanted to be mounted. He wanted a cock in him. He stared at the appealingly big bulge at his mate's crotch, imagining a thick, long cock under that fabric, imagining pulling it out and taking it inside his body. The image nearly made him dizzy with sheer *want*, and he whined, needing it.

A part of him, a very distant part, could feel that there was something wrong with his thoughts. But he seemed unable to think of anything but being bred—and the virile male watching him with hungry eyes. His mate. *(Mate? He didn't have a mate.)*

The moment the restraints on his wrists were gone, Samir was moving, his vision narrowed to the male still restrained to the medical bed.

"Your Highness, wait—you can't—"

Ignoring the noise *(there was someone else there, but he didn't care)*, Samir straddled the male's powerful thighs and fumbled at the dark fabric separating him from his prize. He finally managed to open it and pulled out a hard, throbbing length. The male under him arched, growling and fucking into his hand, his powerful body surging into a sitting position as the restraint on his left wrist was removed.

Someone yelped in pain. "Your Majesty, I'm just trying to help—let me release your other hand—" There was the sound of flesh hitting flesh hard, and then the annoying voice finally shut up, allowing Samir to focus only on his mate. His mate wrapped a muscular arm around him, crushing them together, and Samir moaned in approval, his aching nipples rubbing against the hard chest. There was the annoying fabric in the way again, but the pressure and friction still felt so good, their crotches grinding together. It felt so good, but it still wasn't enough. He wanted more. He wanted his mate's cock. He wanted to be ploughed. Pumped full of his mate's seed.

His mate growled in approval, clearly sensing his thoughts, his hard cock becoming very slick in Samir's hand, ready for the mating. Then he was yanking Samir's pants down, fabric tearing.

Samir squirmed in impatience until he finally felt a hot, hard cock between his naked cheeks. Yes, please. The slippery head bumped against his hole, smearing its lubricant over it. Samir whined desperately, bearing down until the cockhead finally pushed inside him. It was so big. The stretch hurt, but Samir didn't mind. He wanted it. He wanted the cock deeper. He wanted to be filled to the brim.

And then he was.

In one hard thrust, he was fully seated on the enormous cock. A high-pitched noise left his lips, his eyes rolling to the back of his head. So full. So damn full. It was delicious. He was shaking all over, craving more of this feeling, craving to be ploughed and bred.

His mate growled and toppled them over, somehow managing to do it despite his restrained right wrist. His strength sent a sharp spark of arousal and delight through Samir's body.

A strong breeder would produce strong young.
(*Breeder? Young? Something about those thoughts was odd.*)

The brief uncertainty in Samir's mind was wiped away by a hard thrust of the cock in him. He whined, spreading his legs wider. His mate's weight on him was crushing, but it felt so good, to feel so small and helpless as an enormous cock moved inside him, bringing a mix of pain, pleasure, and bone-deep satisfaction. This was right, getting bred. His stomach was going to be round and full with his breeder's seed. The thought sent a huge thrill through his body, and Samir moaned, pushing back on the cock in him, needing it, needing more, deeper, harder. The breeder was grunting on top of him, ploughing him just like he wanted. Almost—almost there—

Whining, Samir grabbed his mate's hard buttocks, keeping him deep inside him as he clenched around the cock in him before an overwhelming wave of pleasure washed over him. "Ah!" he cried out, the strength of his orgasm wiping his mind clean.

His mate groaned and, after a few more thrusts, spilled deep inside him. Samir hummed in approval, reveling in the feeling of wetness and mess. Mmm… hopefully he had been bred.

Bred…

Brod?

He felt the man on top of him go rigid just as Samir's eyes flew open.

They stared at each other in stunned shock before springing apart, both of them cursing. Even the pain in his ass wasn't enough to distract Samir from the enormous, mind-blowing realization that he'd just been fucked by Warrehn'ngh'zaver, a man who hated him and a man he very much didn't like.

"What the fuck was that?" Warrehn bit out, yanking on his fly to get it fixed.

His face hot, Samir couldn't even look at him. He was still trying to fix his own clothes when someone on the floor moaned.

Samir froze, wide-eyed, and stared at the man lying by the bed. It took him a moment to recognize Doctor Jihan. Great. So not only had he fucked his king, he'd fucked him in the presence of one of the most famous healers on the planet.

There was a trickle of blood by the doctor's head. "Are you all right, Doctor?" Samir said, bending down to the poor man and immediately regretting it as a dull pain shot through his ass. He grimaced. He was lucky that males of their species had penises that produced a lot of lubrication or it would have been much, much worse, considering the size of Warrehn's cock.

He fought a blush at the thought, unable to look at Warrehn, who was busy trying to free his wrist.

Doctor Jihan moaned weakly again before slowly sitting up, his hand pressed against the sizable bump on his forehead. "I think so," he said dazedly before his gaze sharpened. He looked from Samir to Warrehn, his eyes widening slightly. "You both seem lucid again. So it worked. Do you remember what happened?"

Samir could barely hold the man's gaze. "There was some kind of attack on us?" he said stiffly. "I don't remember much, but I can make an educated guess that we have been drugged with some kind of aphrodisiac."

"Not an aphrodisiac," the doctor said. "You have been drugged with an alien substance that is known for making the victim false-imprint and sexually fixate on the person they were looking at. Sexual congress seems to have fixed your state."

Giving him a strained smile, Samir glanced around, avoiding looking at Warrehn. "May I leave, then? My mother must be anxious."

The doctor's frown deepened. "I'm sorry, Your Highness, but I must run some tests on you first. We can't be certain that the substance is gone from your system—"

"Do you intend to unlock this sometime today?" Warrehn ground out.

Doctor Jihan flushed and scrambled to help him. "Of course, Your Majesty. My apologies. It was for your own safety, you understand. I was attempting to release you when you—when you rendered me unconscious."

Warrehn didn't look particularly contrite, his face stony. His gaze flicked to Samir over the doctor's shoulder and Samir quickly looked away, unsettled and flustered. He'd had the man's *cock* in him, for fuck's sake. Simple eye contact should have been nothing by comparison.

"Your Majesty, wait—I must insist that I need to run some tests—"

Warrehn walked out.

Letting out a frustrated sigh, Doctor Jihan turned to Samir. "I'm sorry, but I really need to run those tests, Your Highness. The effects of the substance on Calluvians have never been documented, and we cannot be certain that the symptoms have passed permanently and the drug doesn't have lasting effects."

Sighing, Samir sat down on the examination table and submitted himself to what felt like hundreds of different tests.

Unfortunately, Doctor Jihan turned out to be correct. The drug wasn't gone from his system, his hormone levels increasing again.

"Curious," Doctor Jihan murmured, rubbing the bridge of his nose. "I suppose Calluvian cells react differently to the substance and that might be why our biology can't purge it from the system. Or perhaps one intercourse just isn't enough. Normally, the mating season of those primates ends with a successful pregnancy, but I wonder how it will work in this case..." He gave Samir an awkward look. "Forgive me for asking, Your Highness, but it's important. You were on the receiving end of the intercourse, correct?"

Samir gave a clipped nod, refusing to look embarrassed. None of this was his fault.

The doctor hummed, looking back at the readings. "And you never felt the urge to be the aggressor?"

"No," Samir said stiffly.

"Interesting... It was clearly the opposite for His Majesty. I wonder how it works... Why does the substance affect different people differently? Perhaps it has to do with the person's natural inclinations and preferences? Hmm... I wonder if it's connected to one's personality... I suppose we're lucky you and His Majesty had opposite inclinations, or it would have been disastrous."

Lucky? Samir wouldn't call it luck.

"May I go now?" he said tersely.

Doctor Jihan stopped muttering under his breath and studied him carefully. "Do you feel like yourself, Your Highness?"

Samir suppressed a grimace. The examination had lasted for nearly an hour, and as time had passed, Samir had become increasingly aware of the semen still trickling out of his ass. In fact, his thoughts kept fixating on it with alarming frequency—and he was getting vaguely upset that the seed was leaving him. Being *wasted*.

"It's coming back," Samir said with a pinched look. "My thoughts keep wandering to—to wanting to be bred."

"Interesting," Doctor Jihan said, noting something in his datapad. His dry, scientific approach made Samir feel less mortified than he otherwise would have been.

"Can you do something about it?" he said, unable to keep desperation out of his voice. He didn't want to turn back into the mindless creature obsessed with getting bred.

Doctor Jihan shook his head slowly, still looking at the readings in front of him. "Perhaps if I have more time," he said. "And more data. More points of reference."

Samir flushed, realizing what the doctor was implying.

He opened his mouth, to say that he absolutely wasn't going to get fucked by Warrehn'ngh'zaver in order to provide him with his precious data, but unfortunately his thoughts kind of stuck on the concept of getting fucked, need slicing through his system and making his cock harden again.

Fuck.

"All right," Samir said with as much dignity as he could muster. It wasn't a lot. "I trust that no one will find out about this, Doctor."

Doctor Jihan frowned. "Of course, Your Highness. I'm offended you even need to say that. My lips are sealed."

Samir wandered out of the medical wing, his thoughts already beginning to cloud.

By the time he found Warrehn, he could barely think.

Warrehn glared at him from behind his desk.

"Get out," he ground out, his jaw clenched so hard it looked painful.

Licking his dry lips, Samir closed the door and leaned against it. He watched Warrehn watch his every move, blue eyes dark with hunger and hatred, his sun-bronzed face hard as stone.

"I don't want to be here, either," Samir said, his hand gripping the door handle behind him.

"I know you did it," Warrehn said, getting to his feet.

"Did what?" Samir said distractedly, watching Warrehn approach and unable to look away from his powerful muscles and thick thighs. The thick bulge between them. Fuck, he wanted it. He needed it. He needed to be filled again. To be ploughed hard.

"You're the one behind this. You and your snake of a mother." Warrehn grabbed Samir's shoulder and shoved him around to face the door before yanking Samir's pants down.

"Fuck you," Samir said, arching his back and exposing his ass to Warrehn's eyes. Come on, come on, come *on*. "You think I want this?"

"I don't pretend to understand your twisted mind," Warrehn said, his slick cockhead bumping against Samir's sensitive hole.

Samir bit his lip hard to stop himself from whining needily.

Although the doctor had used the dermal regenerator and a muscle relaxant on him, he was still a little sensitive down there. He didn't care. He wanted to be fucked. He wanted to be bred, pumped full of seed.

"Just get on with it," he gritted out, clinging to his sanity with the last remnants of his self-control. "Hope it works this time and we never have to do this again."

"Same," Warrehn grunted before sinking his teeth into Samir's nape and thrusting into him.

And just like that, all his thoughts were gone. There was only the cock in him, deliciously thick and long, ploughing him, owning him, breeding him. Samir couldn't live without it. Didn't want to live without it. It felt like he existed to take that cock and nothing else mattered.

By the time the breeder spilled into him, Samir was nearly-sobbing. The sensation of another man's come filling his hole was enough to push him over the edge. He came, moaning loudly, his body shaking with the aftershocks of pleasure as his hole clenched greedily around the cock in him. It felt glorious.

Then, the fog in his mind cleared. And all he felt was disgust with himself. He shoved Warrehn off him, yanked his pants up, and all but ran out of the room, unable to look at the other man.

He strode toward his rooms, Warrehn's come trickling down his leg with every step he took.

Don't think about it.

The sound of approaching high heels made him cringe and quicken his steps. He just wanted to get to his room and take a dozen showers. And hopefully forget that the whole thing had happened — twice.

"Samir!"

He came to a halt, very reluctantly, allowing his mother to catch up, even though she was about the last person he wanted to see now.

"Was that you?" he said, without looking at her. "It was you, wasn't it?"

He felt Dalatteya's gaze sweep over him from head to toe, no doubt taking in his rumpled clothes. He wondered if he looked as fucked out as he felt.

"It was a mistake," she said quietly, taking his arm and steering him toward his rooms.

"Forgive me, my darling. My orders weren't carried out precisely."

Samir snorted. A mistake. Right. His mother never made mistakes. "What happened to not allowing Emyr's son to lay a finger on me?"

Dalatteya grimaced. "As I said, it was a mistake. A very unfortunate mistake. I didn't plan for this—please believe me. I'm truly sorry." Her lips folded into a thin line as she looked straight ahead. Her voice was very strained when she said, "Are you… all right?"

He was about to scoff, but then he paused. The situation probably brought back bad memories for her. She was a victim of sexual harassment and coercion. It was extremely unlikely that she had planned for Samir to go through a similar ordeal. It seemed it really was an honest mistake, however unlikely it might have seemed.

"I'm fine," he said shortly, hopefully in a tone that made it clear that he had no intention of discussing the matter with his mother.

She laughed, the sound devoid of any humor. "Of course you're not *fine*," she said sharply. "After you had to put up with—with—"

"I don't want to talk about it, Mother. Please at least allow me to keep some of my dignity. I did what I had to. It's not like I had any choice. Hopefully that was the end of it."

She sighed. "I don't think it is."

Samir frowned and looked at her. "Why do you think so?"

Her expression a little tight, Dalatteya pushed the door to Samir's bedroom open and entered it ahead of him. She waited patiently until he closed the door before she spoke again.

"I've just come back from talking to Uriel. Apparently, his supplier mislabeled several substances and sold Uriel the wrong one by mistake. The drug Uriel intended to purchase was basically just a strong aphrodisiac. I gave you an antidote for it, so you shouldn't have been affected. I don't know how the mix-up occurred—and frankly, it doesn't matter now. There are more pressing concerns like the fact that the substance you were drugged with was overdosed. Normally a brief contact of one's skin with the substance would be enough to be significantly affected, but you received at least ten times the recommended dose."

Samir made a face. Just great. Fucking fantastic. "For crying out loud, Mother," he said with a sigh. He had no words. The whole mess was entirely avoidable—and unnecessary. "Was that really necessary?"

His mother didn't even have the grace to look guilty. "Don't look at me that way. You left me with no choice. If you actually made an effort and helped me remove Emyr's son from the picture, none of this would have happened!"

"Yes, it's clearly my fault," Samir said, very dryly. "What were you hoping to achieve by drugging Warrehn that way? It's too damn suspicious."

Dalatteya frowned, rubbing her forehead with one delicate finger. "It wouldn't have been suspicious at all if the substances weren't mixed up and you weren't affected. The original drug I chose has a delayed activation and would have started working forty-two hours after Uriel poisoned the air in the breakfast room, and it's impossible to detect in one's blood after the first few hours. No one would have suspected anything when he attempted to assault you during the publicity tour. *Attempted* being the key word—not this! You would have been perfectly safe all the time."

Samir found himself softening when he saw the genuine distress in his mother's eyes. "I'm fine, Mother," he said, more softly. "It's just sex. Sex means nothing. I can endure it."

She closed her eyes for a moment, her throat working, her telepathic aura still emanating discomfort and distress. "I know you can endure it," she said evenly. "You're my son. You're strong. You've survived worse. But I wish you never knew what it's like to endure such a thing."

Samir swallowed, not knowing what to say.

Before he could figure it out, his mother turned and left.

Chapter 10

Samir had always prided himself on possessing a strong will. He could work on a given task for days without giving in to the urge to sleep and rest, no matter how tedious the task was. He could ignore his physical needs and go long stretches of time without sex. So he had thought he could ignore this artificial need, too.

He had been wrong.

Samir's thoughts started getting clouded barely an hour after his mother had left. He tried to ignore it at first, forcing himself to focus on the education reform he had been working on. Half an hour later, he had to set his datapad aside—he could no longer focus on the words, his mind foggy with inane thoughts and wants. He wanted to be filled. He wanted to be bred again. He still had enough of his mind present that his own thoughts disgusted him, but he couldn't seem to stop thinking that. Couldn't stop wanting that.

He wanted to be bred again. He felt like he fucking needed it, like he would die without it. He kept thinking of Warrehn's cock, huge and red, the fat head glistening with lubricant.

Get a fucking grip.

He made it to two hours before he lost the battle with himself and got to his feet on his shaking legs.

He left the room, barely seeing where he was going, searching for his mate's telepathic presence. He had to stop several times to stroke his cock through the fabric of his trousers, whining softly in frustration. He ended up unfastening his fly and stroking himself desperately as he walked, vaguely registering that the servicing droids were stopping their work and staring at him in befuddlement. He didn't care. He wanted his mate, his breeder. *(He had no such thing, snap out of it, damn it!)* He needed him.

Samir literally stumbled into him in some corridor in the west wing. They stared at each other for one long, charged moment, Warrehn's expression a mix of fury and animal want.

"Damn you," Warrehn ground out before slamming him against the wall and yanking Samir's pants down.

He had him right there, in the middle of the corridor, hard and fast, like a mindless beast satisfying his base urges. He was rough, and it hurt quite a bit, the natural lubricant of Warrehn's cock only doing so much considering his size, but the sting somehow made everything only sharper, hotter, better. Samir couldn't get enough, groaning and pushing back, relishing how heavy and strong the male taking him was. Virile.

He came fast, just from being ploughed like that, but somehow, he still remained hard, not satisfied in the least. He wanted to be full of semen. He needed to be full of semen.

"Your Highness, your mother is looking for you."

The voice failed to penetrate the fog in his head. It was just noise, unimportant. Samir opened his eyes and looked at the droid blearily, his mind blissfully blank as his body shuddered under the force of the other man's thrusts.

He moaned at a particularly well-aimed thrust.

There, deeper.

"Your Highness, Her Excellency said you must come to her office at your earliest convenience—"

"Out of my sight," his mate growled, his hands gripping Samir's hips hard as his cock pistoned in and out of him.

The droid must have listened to him, because everything went blessedly silent, and Samir could finally focus on the glorious sensation of the thick cock taking him. So good. So right.

When his hole was finally filled with seed, it was such a profound relief, the satisfaction of it unbearable. Samir sighed happily, coming again. So good. Such peace and fulfillment.

He wasn't sure how much time had passed when a sigh broke the silence.

"Damn it," a low voice said into his nape. It sounded defeated.

Samir opened his eyes and stared at the wall in front of him blankly as Warrehn's softening cock slipped out of him. Goddammit.

"At least it was two hours this time," he said, looking for a silver lining.

Warrehn said nothing, his telepathic presence dark and oppressive. It made the hairs on the back of Samir's neck stand up, as if there were a predator behind him. An angry one.

"It is good," Samir said, pulling his pants up. "It was barely an hour last time."

"You're very calm about this. But then again, of course you are."

"What is that supposed to mean?" Samir said, lifting his chin and turning to Warrehn.

It was jarring to see him completely dressed, as if nothing had happened, as if Samir didn't feel Warrehn's come leaking down his leg. "I just see little point in bitching about something we can't change. There's always the bright side."

"Right," Warrehn said, very dryly, putting his hands into the pockets of his dark jacket. "The bright side being that you and your mother accomplished whatever you were aiming for. What was it again, exactly?"

Samir could only look at him, hating that he couldn't even truthfully say that Warrehn was wrong. The whole thing *had* been his mother's doing, however inadvertently. "My mother would never willingly put me in a situation where I have to get intimate with Emyr's son," he said at last. That much was true. "She hated him more than anything, and she hates you by extension."

Warrehn's lips curled into something that wasn't quite a smile. "Yes, she hated him so much that she pretty much lived in his rooms. I couldn't visit my father's rooms without stumbling into my dear auntie."

"That doesn't signify," Samir said. "He forced her."

Warrehn shrugged, raking a hand through his lush golden-brown hair. It made Samir's fingers twitch. It was positively unfair that such a grim, hard man had such gorgeous hair. It looked so soft.

"He might well have, but from what I've seen, either your mother is an exceptionally good actress or she enjoyed kissing a man she loathed."

"That means nothing," Samir said, hiding his confusion. "I strongly dislike you. But I enjoyed fucking you, even if it was the drug's doing, so what? It doesn't change my feelings about you. You're still a grumpy, judgmental prick I don't like."

Warrehn's brows drew together. "The situations aren't comparable. My father didn't drug your mother with an aphrodisiac-like substance. Every emotion she felt for him was her own, whether she hated him or wanted him. It's fucked up if she can't see the irony of this situation and her hypocrisy. She's now no better than the man she claims to despise. He took her consent away. She took away mine."

"Whataboutism is pathetic and doesn't make the horrible things she has suffered through okay," Samir said before adding belatedly, "And my mother has nothing to do with this."

Warrehn shook his head. "You're a far shittier liar than she is. Seriously, don't bother. I'm not buying your innocent act." He looked at Samir flatly, his finely shaped, sensual lips twisting into something ugly. "What I don't understand is what your goal is. You can't seriously think a few fucks would make me forget all the things your family has done to mine. Sorry, but your hole isn't that good."

Samir punched him in the mouth.

He felt a moment of vicious satisfaction when he saw a trickle of blood run down from Warrehn's split lip. But his satisfaction was short-lived.

Warrehn grabbed his wrist and shoved it against the wall. Leaning down, he glowered at Samir, his forearm pressing hard against Samir's wrist.

Samir glared back, inhaling shakily. It was a struggle to breathe, his lungs full of Warrehn's scent. "Let go," he growled. "You deserved that. You should be *thanking* me for the privilege."

"Privilege?" Warrehn said, his eyes glinting nastily. "If you and your mother resort to using your body to achieve your dubious ends, that's unlikely to be a rare privilege."

"You asshole," Samir hissed, trying to yank his hand free and punch him again, to no avail. He was all but spitting, he was so furious. "I loathe you, you utter piece of shit. If your father was half as infuriating as you are, now I understand why he's dead."

Warrehn raised his eyebrows. "So you're finally admitting that your mother killed him."

"I'm admitting no such thing," Samir said, stomping on Warrehn's shoe viciously.

A grimace crossed Warrehn's face, but his grip on Samir's wrist didn't loosen at all. "Tell me what your game is," he said, his gaze roaming over Samir's face, lingering on his panting lips before snapping back to Samir's eyes. "What were you hoping to accomplish by drugging me with that drug?"

"You're the genius who came to this conclusion," Samir said. "You tell me."

"I'm afraid my mind isn't as twisted and slippery as yours. If I can't see a purpose, it doesn't mean it doesn't exist."

"So you admit you aren't as smart as us."

"I admit that I'm not half as underhanded and manipulative as you are. I'm actually an honest person."

Samir laughed. "Get off your high horse, *Your Majesty*. You have no problem with publicly associating with me, the son of the woman who murdered your parents, according to you. If you were so principled, you'd kick us out of your home, public opinion be damned. I guess you're an 'honest person' only when it suits you."

And with that, he yanked his wrist from Warrehn's grip and strode away, trying very hard not to limp.

Fuck him. Seriously, fuck him.

He'd never met a more infuriating, high-handed, self-righteous man!

"I hate you," he muttered viciously, imagining punching Warrehn in his straight perfect nose and then each of his blue eyes, and then his firm mouth, and then burying his hand in that stupidly lush hair and *yanking*, until it hurt.

Fuck, he'd never hated anyone more.

Chapter 11

"I'm sorry, Your Majesty, but we can't cancel the publicity tour," Ayda said, frowning. "Your visit to the provinces has been publicly announced, and canceling it would be bad press you very much don't need."

Warrehn said nothing, looking out the window of his office, his hands in his pockets.

Sirri eyed him curiously from her seat in the corner of the room. She had never seen such tension in Warrehn's body. He was so rigid and tense she could feel it with her skin, despite the distance between them.

"Is it really that bad?" she said, keeping her voice mild. Normally, she took delight in irritating Warrehn, but she could feel it would be a bad idea right now. Warrehn was a high-level telepath, his raw power dangerous even to her. Seriously pissing him off when he was this wound up was a terrible idea.

"What do you think?" Warrehn said, his profile hard and unyielding, as was his tall, powerful body.

Sirri allowed herself to take a moment to appreciate his physique. Warrehn might be a grumpy, miserable prick, but he was a hot one. In a I'm-not-impressed-with-you-and-I'll-fuck-you-up way. It was a pity he wasn't into women. She wouldn't mind a fuck with him, her issues with him notwithstanding. Though rumor had it, he fucked rougher than she preferred.

"Personally, screwing the perfect Prince Samir wouldn't be a hardship," Sirri said with a grin. "The guy is hot, though I'm not sure how I'd feel about fucking a man so much more beautiful than I am. I'm too vain for that."

Ayda hid an amused smile behind her hand, and Sirri winked at her, making the woman blush a little. Huh. Ayda was kind of hot. Maybe she should try to get into her panties before leaving for Tai'Lehr tomorrow.

"He isn't beautiful," Warrehn said, his voice dark.

Sirri raised her eyebrows. "Is there something wrong with your eyesight? The guy is ridiculously gorgeous."

"Beauty comes from the inside. He's ugly, no matter how lovely he looks."

Sirri scoffed, rolling her eyes. "Please. Since when have you men ever cared about inner beauty and all that rot when it comes to getting your dicks wet? Don't tell me it was a hardship to fuck him—I won't believe you."

She noted curiously that Warrehn's hand clenched inside his pocket.

"I barely remember anything," he said flatly. "When the drug takes over, I feel like I'm possessed." He looked at Ayda. "You can't seriously expect me to go on that publicity tour in this state. I can barely go a few hours before the symptoms become overwhelming."

Ayda winced. "It's not ideal, but we have no choice. Canceling the tour a day after it was announced would only make you look fickle and unreliable. It seems the interval between—between the spikes of symptoms has been getting longer, correct?"

Warrehn gave a clipped nod.

"See, it'll be all right," Ayda said with a smile, but even she didn't sound all that sure.

"Could you leave us alone, please?" Sirri asked her.

"Of course," Ayda said. She looked at Warrehn and bowed. "Your Majesty."

He didn't even glance at her.

"You're so rude," Sirri said when the door closed behind Ayda.

He didn't say anything, his handsome face grim and closed-off.

Sighing, Sirri walked over and put her hand on his shoulders. "War, listen," she said, looking him in the eyes. "In all seriousness, I get it: he's the son of your parents' murderer and it must be disgusting to come to your senses and find yourself balls deep in him—I really get it. But beating yourself up over something you have no control over is pointless. Loosen up. You're so tense I feel like I'm standing next to a bomb that's about to go off. Let it go. *It isn't your fault.* Your attraction to him isn't real."

Warrehn averted his gaze, a muscle jumping in his cheek as he clenched his jaw.

Sirri stared at him, stunned. "You want him," she said slowly as the realization hit. Although she had tried to rile him up about ogling Prince Samir on the court day, it had been a *joke*. She hadn't truly thought Warrehn wanted Dalatteya's son, knowing his deep hatred for her and anything hers. "You wanted him before the whole ordeal."

He glared at her, the force of it making her want to step back. She gritted her teeth and stayed where she was. She wouldn't back off just because he was a man twice her size and could do some serious damage to her brain if he wanted to.

"It was a superficial, fleeting attraction I would have never acted on," he said.

She wasn't sure she believed him. He was being too defensive, too guilty and stressed over the whole thing for it to be some superficial attraction.

But for his sake, she hoped he wasn't lying.

Because if he really wanted Dalatteya's son… it would be a disaster of epic proportions.

Before she could say anything, he said with a sigh, "I need some air."

He walked out, leaving her highly unsettled.

And scared.

****

Warrehn stared at the surface of the lake unseeingly.

If you were so principled, you'd kick us out of your home, public opinion be damned.

Damn him. Even more than an hour later, despite his meeting with the publicist and Sirri, those dark blue eyes glaring at him hatefully were still at the forefront of his mind.

I guess you're an "honest person" only when it suits you.

Warrehn threw a pebble into the lake and watched it bounce a few times before sinking into the unknown depths. He felt a little like that, too. Drowning, unsure where the way up was.

Away from Samir and his disconcerting effect on him, Warrehn could see that he'd behaved like a toxic ass around him. The things he'd said—he'd never said stuff like that to men he'd fucked, even when they were actual professional whores. But around Samir it was like he couldn't control what was coming out of his mouth at all.

He had *burned* to put Samir in his place—and that place was beneath him, in every way that mattered.

His own obsessive, toxic thoughts disturbed him.

Maybe it was the drug. A side effect, one of many. Just like the itchy feeling building under his skin right now. Growing. Wanting.

Warrehn took in a deep, calming breath. It had been just an hour and a half. He had better self-control than that. Samir was Dalatteya's son, and everything that entailed. He was treacherous and poisonous, no matter how gorgeous he was or how pretty his pink lips looked.

They'd look even better wrapped around his cock as Samir choked on it, looking up at him with wet, pleading eyes.

Warrehn gritted his teeth, his cock aching.

His communicator went off and he answered, glad for the distraction. He needed all the distraction in the world right now. "Yes?" he bit off.

"I was going to ask if everything was fine, but it seems the answer is no," Rohan said dryly.

Warrehn took another deep breath and let it out slowly, his shoulders relaxing at the sound of his friend's voice—though Rohan was more of a brother than a friend. They had grown up together ever since Warrehn had become an unwilling guest in Rohan's home. Warrehn might have resented Rohan's father for not letting him leave Tai'Lehr, but he could never bring himself to resent Rohan when he was always there for him, an older brother figure who had remained patient with him despite Warrehn's numerous attempts to escape.

"I know you want to go home," an eighteen-year-old Rohan had said a year into Warrehn's involuntary stay on Tai'Lehr, his black eyes solemn as he held Warrehn's gaze. "I get it that you want to avenge your family. But look: escaping is pointless. You're just eleven. No one will take your accusations seriously. You're a child in the eyes of the law—and you'd be entirely in the regent's power even if you were to return home. Wait until you're old enough—but use that time wisely. Dalatteya'il'zaver is said to be a very smart, cunning woman. She'll crush you politically right now if you go back as a child or she will just have you killed. You'll need to learn how to be heard if you want to succeed when you go back."

When. The fact that even back then Rohan had said *when* was the single most reassuring thought Warrehn had chosen to fixate on. After that conversation, he'd stopped trying to escape. He'd followed Rohan's advice and forced himself to learn social sciences, everything a king should know to rule effectively, single-minded in his purpose. He would go back and he would avenge his family. And he would find and get his little brother back.

It was gutting that he'd accomplished neither. He still had no proof of Dalatteya's guilt; instead, he was forced to play politics and put up with her presence in his home. And he might have found his little brother, but he had lost him again. Eridan had chosen to leave. He was gone, as good as dead. Members of the High Hronthar were forbidden from being involved in politics, so Eridan returning to the monastery had effectively removed him from the line of succession. He might still be a prince, but it was an empty title now. Eridan had chosen a life with that manipulative, treacherous asshole to a life Warrehn had offered him.

A wave of bitterness and loneliness washed over him.

"Did you expect me to be in a good mood given the situation?" Warrehn said, pushing those thoughts away. There was no use dwelling on them. He was fine on his own. He didn't need anyone.

"You tell me," Rohan said. "That was a shitty thing to do to message me that you've been drugged and then ignore all my messages and calls. What the fuck, War? What happened? Are you hurt?"

Warrehn glanced at his crotch and pulled a face. "I would have preferred to be."

"What?"

Pinching the bridge of his nose, Warrehn explained.

It took him nearly half an hour. It didn't help that by the end of it, he could barely focus on the conversation, his attention drifting to Samir with aggravating frequency.

When he was done, silence reigned.

"I don't understand her motivation," Rohan said, sounding puzzled.

"Me neither. But it doesn't matter. I just need to get this drug out of my system."

"I think learning her motivation matters. If we don't figure out what she's hoping to accomplish by this, you might play right into her hands no matter what you do. Maybe the drug is just a means to an end and it's your reaction she wants. Please don't make any rash decisions, War."

Warrehn grimaced. He knew Rohan was right. He had no proof that she was guilty of anything. Samir being affected too messed it all up, making her involvement seem unlikely. No matter how badly he wanted to officially accuse the viper of drugging him, he had to think of whether it would play into her hands and how it would look to the public.

I guess you're an "honest person" only when it suits you.

Warrehn bit the inside of his cheek, hating how much Samir's words had gotten under his skin. Hating that he wasn't wrong.

"It's baffling," Rohan said. "I just can't see why she would drug her own son. Is it possible that she thinks you might fall for him?"

Warrehn laughed. "If she's hoping for that, she's an idiot," he said. "That'll never happen."

Rohan hummed and fell silent for a moment. "Did you fuck him?"

Warrehn glared at the lake's still surface.

"Of course I did," he said irritably.

"And? Was it good?"

"What kind of question is that?" Warrehn said. "Don't you feel good when you fuck someone?"

"There's no need to get so defensive," Rohan said.

His placating tone was infuriating.

Warrehn closed his eyes and breathed slowly. "I'm not being defensive," he said with forced calm. "I'm just a little frustrated. You would be too, if your balls were blue for nearly two hours. Even talking to you is—hard. It's hard to focus."

Rohan made a sympathetic sound. "All right. I won't keep you, then. I'll consult with our doctors. Maybe we can find a solution Doctor Jihan has overlooked."

Warrehn grunted in affirmative and ended the call.

Running a hand over his eyes, he breathed in, and out. "A little frustrated" was an understatement. He'd never been so sexually frustrated in his life. He was a man in his prime with a healthy appetite for sex, but this was ridiculous even by his standards. He was this close to just getting his cock out and jacking himself off out here in the open, potential witnesses and consequences be damned. The worst part was, he knew it wouldn't work anyway. He didn't want to just get off. He wanted to stick his cock into Dalatteya's son, fuck him up, and *breed* him. The strength of that desire made him angry, disgusted, and frustrated in equal measure.

Rationally, he knew Sirri was right and feeling this wasn't his fault. While it was true that he had been attracted to Samir prior to being dosed with the drug, it had been a fleeting attraction any healthy man would feel to an exquisitely handsome young thing. He would have never acted on it.

And now… no matter what he told himself, the fact was, he *burned* to fuck the son of his family's murderer—and he'd fucked him already, several times, and burned to do it again. It was infuriating, the knowledge that he wasn't strong enough to resist the pull—that Dalatteya had once again outplayed him, whatever her game was.

The question was, had Samir known of her plans? Warrehn hadn't been able to sense dishonesty when he'd briefly read Samir's surface thoughts. Samir had seemed as surprised by the air-poisoning as he had been. It didn't necessarily mean he was unaware of his mother's plans, but Warrehn didn't dare delve deeper into his mind because of how compatible their minds were. He didn't want to be influenced by their natural compatibility.

It was bad enough that the drug was already affecting his judgment somewhat. Although Rohan's suggestion that Dalatteya might be expecting him to fall for her son was laughable, it was true that he didn't hate Samir as much as he hated his mother. Whether it was the drug's influence or not, he didn't know. He was frustrated and angered by the situation and behaved like a toxic ass around Samir, but it wasn't true hatred. He hated Dalatteya. His feelings for her son were far more complex.

It didn't help that Samir looked like a fucking fairytale prince: luscious violet hair, deep blue eyes, milky skin, and pretty pink lips. He was all grace and poise, making Warrehn feel like a rough, uncivilized oaf next to him. Samir *was* drop-dead gorgeous. Even before the drug debacle, Warrehn had had a few fleeting fantasies of forcing Samir to his knees in the throne room and making him suck his cock in front of Dalatteya and the entire court.

The cock in question throbbed, and Warrehn hissed in frustration.

Damn it.

Picking up his communicator, he found Samir's number in the royal database and pressed Connect.

"It's been two hours," Warrehn said when Samir answered.

"Yes," Samir said. He sounded a little wary—and a little breathless.

"The drug is clearly wearing off, but not fast enough. We should test how long we can go before giving in."

"We?"

Warrehn sighed. "Yes. The publicity tour can't be canceled, so we need to work together, for the time being, and figure out our limits. We'll coordinate our comings and goings until the drug wears off."

"All right," Samir said, sounding a little stunned.

Warrehn almost smiled. People mistakenly thought he wasn't capable of being rational, but he was very much capable of it—when it suited him. If he didn't approach this situation rationally, he knew he would fucking explode from sheer frustration.

"This is what we will do," Warrehn said. "You will message me every half an hour and report on how you're doing. If your—condition gets unbearable, you will tell me. I'll do the same. The trick is to find our limits without pushing them. I don't want to touch you more often than I have to."

"I assure you the sentiment is entirely mutual."

"Good," Warrehn said, throwing another pebble into the lake. It sank immediately—too much force. "So we understand each other. I expect a message every half an hour."

He hung up, glanced down at the tent in his pants, and grimaced. To say he wasn't looking forward to finding out his limits was putting it mildly.

The first message came exactly half an hour later. *It's still bearable.*

Warrehn wasn't sure he agreed. But he typed, *Same.*

The second message was the same.

Warrehn was absolutely lying as he replied that he was similarly fine. He wasn't. His concentration was completely shot, his hands trembling so badly he had to ball them into fists.

But he refused to be the one to give in first.

Thankfully, Samir's next message came much sooner. *I can't stand it anymore. Come to my room.*

Warrehn had never moved so fast. He covered the distance to the palace in record time and strode past the startled servants and robots. He had no idea if anyone witnessed him entering Samir's rooms—and truth be told, he didn't care.

Samir was on his bed, his weight on his elbows and knees, his beautiful ass in the air. The small, pink hole between those round, creamy cheeks made Warrehn's mouth water. He felt like an animal seeing a fertile bitch in heat. The urge to breed him was overwhelming, even though rationally he knew it was impossible.

"Just do it," Samir whispered hoarsely into the mattress, without looking at him. "Fill me up."

And Warrehn did.

Chapter 12

They departed for the publicity tour early in the morning.

Samir wasn't used to traveling in land vehicles. It was a little too old-fashioned for his tastes. But he had to admit the vintage car Warrehn's people had chosen was very impressive and comfortable. It was pretty big, with lots of space and everything they needed: a dining area equipped with a teleporting service—they could order anything and the meal would be delivered to them—two beds, a bathroom with a sonic shower, and a small living room area. The car was soundproof and the windows were one-way, giving them privacy—a much-needed feature, considering what they were up to.

Their days went like this:

Samir usually woke up with Warrehn's cock already inside him, ploughing him hard. He lay there, half-asleep, luxuriating in the feeling of being taken by a virile male in his prime and being pumped full of his seed. When he came, they sprang apart, avoiding each other's eyes, and retreated to the opposite ends of the vehicle until it was time for their first stop of the day.

It was incredibly jarring to put an impassive, polite mask on his face around Warrehn and call him His Majesty, as if he hadn't had Warrehn's cock in him a short while ago—as if he wasn't already eager for more.

Not that *Samir* was eager for more. It was the drug, not him.

After all the smiling and baby-kissing, they were back in the car. By that time, Samir was trembling with impatience and want, but they didn't fuck unless absolutely necessary—which was usually when one of them couldn't stand it anymore and gave in. To Samir's embarrassment and annoyance, more often than not, he was the desperate one. It was utterly unfair, because Doctor Jihan had said the concentration of the drug was higher in Warrehn's system. Samir had a sneaking suspicion that Warrehn, as a high-level telepath, used advanced meditative techniques to control himself.

The worst part was, the more time passed, the clearer Samir's head was during sex. The sex was no longer a hazy coupling he could barely remember afterward; he could now remember *things*. He could remember the way he clung to Warrehn, begging for more of his cock, begging for deeper and harder. He could remember the utterly embarrassing way he often behaved during sex, pulling Warrehn on top of him and refusing to let go until he gave him what he needed—which was a cock stuffed into him as often as possible. He could remember the particularly mortifying occasion of Warrehn's publicist walking in on them a few days ago. She had frozen in the doorway, her eyes wide, before stepping back and slamming the car's door shut. That had been so awkward—Samir couldn't look Ayda in the eye for days.

Usually they made another stop in the afternoon at some charity function or hospital. Their PR teams tried hard not to let those events go on for more than a few hours, but sometimes it couldn't be helped. And those times were the *worst*.

Samir could only sit there, desperate and aching, and stare hungrily at the man beside him, digging his fingernails into his own thighs to stop himself from climbing into Warrehn's lap and yanking his fly open.

Afterward, Samir usually found himself riding the king's cock in a restroom, fast and hard, so desperate for it he didn't give a damn that the flimsy door was the only thing separating them from the crowd of reporters and mamas with their babies. Later, he would be beyond mortified, but that would be much later. The damned drug didn't leave room for rational thought when all he wanted was Warrehn's cock. It was fucking horrible. Samir had never had so much sex in his life—had never wanted sex so much.

Miraculously, they'd managed not to get caught despite all the occasions they'd fucked in public and semi-public places. Either that, or their PR teams deserved a big raise.

When night fell, they slept in the same bed. It was just practical: they'd learned the hard way that it was very difficult to function on only a few hours of uninterrupted sleep if they had to get up for sex several times at night. It was more practical to sleep in the same bed. That way, Samir didn't even have to fully wake up: Warrehn just pressed him into the mattress, half-awake himself, and pushed his slick cock into him.

Middle-of-the-night sex was usually more unhurried—sometimes Samir didn't even awaken—but sometimes the desire for sex was so urgent, he woke up utterly desperate for cock. He would climb on top of Warrehn, find his stiff cock, and sink onto it with a blissed-out moan. He would ride himself to completion, and then beyond, until he finally got his hole full of Warrehn's seed.

Then he would fall on top of Warrehn and sleep like the dead.

They were on the road for fifteen days when Samir woke up and realized that they *hadn't* had sex at night.

"What is it?" Warrehn said, his voice still rough from sleep. He was lying on his back, his naked body large and muscular but somehow graceful too. He reminded Samir of a cat. A wild, big cat with a golden-brown mane that looked amazingly soft and messy right now. One blue eye blinked open when Samir didn't say anything.

Samir found himself blushing when he realized that he had been staring. But who would blame him? He had eyes and Warrehn was a fine specimen of a man when he wasn't talking.

"We didn't have sex last night," Samir said, clearing his throat a little.

Warrehn's eyebrows drew together. "Are you sure?" he said, rubbing at his stubbled jaw. "Maybe we slept through it. Wouldn't be the first time."

"I'm quite sure," Samir said dryly. It was pretty hard not to notice a lack of come in his asshole. "You aren't exactly small. I always feel it in the morning."

"Let me check," Warrehn said, and before Samir realized what he meant, he was between Samir's legs, spreading his thighs and looking at him.

Samir flushed, trying to close his thighs. "Stop that," he hissed. He'd never had anyone look at him down there, not so up-close.

"Don't be ridiculous, let me look," Warrehn said, but paused and looked at him. "Are you *embarrassed*?"

Samir glared at him with as much dignity as he could muster. It was difficult, considering that his face felt on fire and Warrehn's head was between his thighs and the view was making it hard to focus.

"Of course not," he said, trying to appear more experienced than he actually was.

Warrehn narrowed his eyes. "You've had sex before this, right? Before me?"

"Of course I have," Samir said stiffly.

"How many times?"

"Why does it matter?"

Warrehn's fingers gripped his thighs harder, not hard enough to hurt, but hard enough to make him pay attention. "How many times?"

"Four," Samir grumbled. It was technically closer to three, because he had left after a handjob the first time, but four sounded more impressive. He wasn't sure why he even wanted to impress Warrehn with his sexual prowess, but he could tell Warrehn was a lot more experienced than him, and it bothered him for some reason.

"Four," Warrehn repeated, and there was something in his voice that sounded… skeptical? Baffled?

Samir darted his eyes to him. "What?" he said, lifting his chin. "How many times have *you* had sex?"

Although Warrehn didn't smile, something in his eyes told Samir that he wanted to. "More than four," he said mildly, somehow managing to sound insufferably superior.

Samir glowered at him, but before he could say anything, Warrehn moved his head down and *licked* between his thighs. Samir jerked as if electrocuted. "Stop—what are you doing—" he said breathlessly, grabbing Warrehn's hair. "No—Ah! Ah! Don't stop…"

That was how he'd found out that he absolutely loved having his asshole licked. *Eaten out*, as Warrehn said. They did it all the time after that morning, but Samir had mixed feelings about the whole thing, no matter how much he loved it. The problem was, it served *no* purpose. Samir couldn't blame his desire to be eaten out on the drug. The drug made him want Warrehn's cock—Warrehn's seed—in him. This was… just sex. Mind-blowing, addictive sex they shouldn't be having.

But Samir didn't voice his doubts aloud. He wasn't sure Warrehn had noticed the difference, and if he hadn't, Samir didn't want to be the one pointing it out. As long as they didn't speak about it, they could carry on as they were and Samir could get his ass eaten every day.

Fuck, Warrehn had turned him into a slut.

***

By the time the publicity tour was over, Samir had had twenty times more sex than he'd had before that, and yet he and Warrehn had barely spoken beyond the same old arguments about Dalatteya and Samir's role in the whole mess. Not that their arguments stopped them from fucking—far from it.

"I'm so glad you're finally back, darling," his mother said, hugging him tightly when they arrived back at the palace.

Samir returned the hug, smiling. He'd missed her. She smelled familiar but kind of weird. It took him a moment to realize why: he'd gotten used to smelling Warrehn's aftershave when he was touched.

"Let's go inside," Dalatteya said, tucking her arm into his and leading him away.

Samir glanced back at Warrehn, who was speaking to his publicist outside the vehicle. Samir frowned as he turned away, feeling a little strange.

After nearly a month in close quarters with Warrehn, Samir was used to feeling Warrehn's telepathic presence all the time and it felt… odd to walk away from him.

He shook his head. It was probably natural. Forced proximity and lots of physical contact would do it.

"How are you, sweetheart?" Dalatteya said, squeezing his arm.

Samir smiled thinly, knowing what she was really asking about. "It's better, Mother. It's not as bad as it used to be."

It was true. By the end of the tour, they could go up to seven hours without sex and sometimes didn't even have sex at night. They still slept in the same bed because— because it was easier not to have to get up for morning sex.

The relief was plain on his mother's face. "I'm glad. Do you think it'll be over soon? Doctor Jihan hasn't made any progress on the antidote."

Samir shrugged, unsure what to say. While the frequency of spikes of need had decreased, he'd found himself spacing out a disturbing number of times lately, just looking at Warrehn and wanting his hands and mouth on him. He wasn't sure what to think of it. He hadn't mentioned the new symptom in his video calls with Doctor Jihan, feeling too awkward, especially considering that Warrehn was right there.

"It'll probably go away on its own," he said, glancing back at Warrehn again.

The king finally looked at him over Ayda's shoulder, and their eyes met. Warrehn frowned, accepting his black mantle from a servant and shrugging it on, his eyes still on Samir.

Samir's stomach clenched.

"Samir?"

Dragging his gaze away, Samir looked back at his mother.

She had a wrinkle between her brows as she glanced at Warrehn and then at him.

"Yes, Mother?" Samir said, feeling a surge of discomfort. He felt as if she'd caught him doing something wrong.

"Nothing, darling," she said after a moment, steering him away.

Quashing the urge to look back at Warrehn again, Samir followed his mother into the palace.

It was good to be home.

Hopefully everything would be back to normal soon.

Chapter 13

The chime of Warrehn's communicator didn't even register at first, all of Samir's senses focused on the cock pounding into him fast. He was moaning quietly as Warrehn grunted on top of him, the massive cock in him pumping in and out of his hole with obscene, slippery sounds. So good. So perfect.

The communicator chimed again.

"Don't you dare," Samir said, grabbing Warrehn's hips and urging him to keep moving.

Warrehn groaned and kept thrusting, but he also reached for his communicator and pressed the accept button, putting the call on speaker. "Yes?" he grunted by Samir's ear, breathing hard. Samir could feel that he was very close, and the thought elicited a sharp wave of arousal through his body. He wanted Warrehn's seed, wanted to be full of it.

"War, I spoke to Idhron about removing the mind traps in Dalatteya's mind so we could read her mind," someone said. The voice was familiar—it was Warrehn's friend, Rohan—but Samir could barely register the meaning as he arched his body and pushed back on the thick cock inside him. Fuck, so damn good. After more than a month of this, he still couldn't get enough.

Warrehn grunted. "And?" he said, thrusting into Samir steadily.

"Idhron said I was wrong: he wasn't the one who placed those mind traps, so he can't remove them. They existed in her mind long before Idhron started brainwashing her."

Warrehn went still. "What?"

Samir whined, wrapping his legs around Warrehn's hips and digging his heels in. He wanted more. Why had Warrehn stopped?

"Move," Samir demanded, uncaring of the significance of the conversation. He knew he should care—a distant part of him told him to pay attention—but it was hard to pay attention when all he wanted was to be filled up and screwed into the mattress. "Come on," he said, trying to push back onto the cock in him. "Need you."

Warrehn shuddered, his eyes becoming unfocused with animal want again. He resumed moving, hard and fast.

Samir moaned in approval.

"What the hell—are you seriously fucking him while you're talking to me? Never mind. Call me later."

Warrehn grunted, his glassy eyes still fixed on Samir's naked body, on Samir's hard, leaking cock nearly touching his stomach, before moving to the place their bodies were connected. He stared at his own cock thrusting in and out of Samir's hole with a strange sort of fascination before looking back at Samir's pleasure-drunk face. "Fuck, look how much you love this…" He shook his head dazedly. "I hate this goddamn drug," he muttered, his voice low and absent, his large hand stroking Samir's pale thigh reverently.

Making an affirmative noise, Samir looped his arms around Warrehn's neck and pulled him down, wanting his mouth on him.

Warrehn obliged him, kissing down his neck, and sucking hickeys there.

This was fairly new for them. Samir wasn't sure why they'd started doing more than sticking Warrehn's cock into his hole, but it felt good, so what difference did it make?

Warrehn sucked hard on his neck, Samir's entire body singing with satisfaction that got sharper and better with every powerful thrust. Warrehn pinched his nipple, and Samir moaned and came. His orgasm caught him completely off-guard, just a bigger wave of pleasure that made him feel like he was floating. He rode it with hitched, blissed-out sighs, stroking Warrehn's hard buttocks and back as the other man came inside him.

"So good," he mumbled.

Warrehn's mouth trailed up his neck, his stubble scratching his smooth skin. Samir smiled, rubbing his nose against Warrehn's prickly cheek.

Suddenly, Warrehn's entire body went rigid. He rolled off Samir with a curse and reached for his communicator. "Rohan," he barked out, completely ignoring Samir now. "What did you say about Dalatteya? If the adepts of the High Hronthar didn't put those traps in her mind, who did?"

Samir frowned and sat up, too. The pleasure induced fog in his head was gone now, and he suddenly recalled what Rohan had said during his call.

Someone else had messed with his mother's mind—someone who wasn't part of the High Hronthar.

"We aren't sure," Rohan said. "I still don't exactly trust Idhron, but Eridan made him promise that he was telling the truth this time. Personally, I'm inclined to believe him. He has no reason to lie about it."

A deep crease appeared between Warrehn's brows. "What exactly did Idhron say?"

"Idhron pretty much admitted that he brainwashed Dalatteya into thinking that Eridan was dead and into liking the kid enough not to be a threat to him when he returned. A few years ago, he also planted into her mind the knowledge that you were on Tai'Lehr, so that she could do the dirty work for him and have you killed and Eridan could ascend to the throne. That's where the assassination attempts on you came from."

Samir's stomach turned. This was the first time he was hearing of this. He distinctly remembered his mother claiming that she'd had no idea about Warrehn's survival. So that had been a lie.

Unlike him, Warrehn seemed unbothered—or maybe because it wasn't news to him. "That's it?" he said, raking a hand through his thick hair, the muscles of his wide back flexing.

Samir dragged his eyes away and looked down at his lap as he waited for Rohan's answer.

"Idhron also admitted that he created a trap in her mind that was supposed to spring if someone tried to search her mind for information about the High Hronthar or Warrehn. But he says there are other traps in her mind, protecting the blocks of her memories he wasn't able to access. They're the ones preventing you from delving deeper into her mind, and Idhron can't remove them, because he isn't the one who put them there."

Samir bit his lip to prevent himself from speaking. Rohan might have known who Warrehn had been having sex with, but it was another thing to speak and acknowledge it aloud. Not to mention that if he said something, Warrehn might actually remember that he was still in the room and take the communicator off speaker.

"He's allegedly the best mind adept on the planet," Warrehn said flatly. "And I'm supposed to believe he wasn't able to access those blocked memories?"

Rohan snorted. "My thoughts exactly. I think he's telling the truth about the mind traps, but he may not be telling us everything he knows."

Sighing, Warrehn grunted, "I don't trust him. Just because he's good to my brother it doesn't make him a decent person. Eridan is the only thing he cares about besides power."

Huh. So could those rumors about Eridan be true? About him and the Grandmaster of the High Hronthar?

Warrehn looked back at him, as if only then realizing that he wasn't alone in the room.

Samir gave him his best innocent look.

Warrehn's blue eyes lingered on his mouth, which probably looked red and puffy from all the times Samir had to bite his lips in order not to moan.

"War?" Rohan said. "Are you there?"

His shoulders tensing, Warrehn turned away again. "Yes," he said tersely. "I'll get to the bottom of it. Thanks for letting me know." He ended the call, but not a moment later, his communicator chimed again.

It was Eridan this time.

"I'm coming back to the palace," he said. "Tonight."

Warrehn straightened up. "You've changed your mind?" he said hoarsely.

"No," Eridan said. He sounded annoyed. "I'm just teaching Castien a lesson. He didn't tell me he was responsible for those assassination attempts on you."

"Are you really surprised?" Warrehn said, chuckling.

Eridan let out a humorless laugh. "I mean, not really. I know my Master and what he's capable of. I'm mostly annoyed that he didn't tell me about it until now. I'll stay for a bit in the palace so that he grovels a little before I take him back. I can stay, right?"

"Of course," Warrehn said, his voice rough. "You're always welcome, Eri. This is your home."

When he ended the call, he turned back to Samir and looked at him with inscrutable blue eyes. "Go to your own room. I don't want Eridan to find out about" —he gestured between them— "this. Stay away while he's visiting. Don't let me catch even a glimpse of you. I'll find you myself when it gets bad."

Feeling irked for reasons he chose not to examine too closely, Samir said, "Fine." He reached for his clothes and dressed quickly. He thought he could feel Warrehn's eyes on him, but when he looked back, Warrehn wasn't looking at him.

Pursing his lips tightly, Samir strode out of the room.

He wasn't even sure why he was so pissed. He just… He supposed he'd just gotten used to them sleeping in one bed and it pissed him off that Warrehn had dismissed him like a used thing. Something unimportant.

Something he was ashamed of.

Chapter 14

The next day, Samir told his mother about the traps in her mind.

Dalatteya's face paled for a moment before she regained her usual composure. "Don't worry about it, darling," she said, her gaze distant and thoughtful. "I'll handle it."

"How? You can't exactly go to the High Hronthar with this problem."

His mother shook her head. "Not to the High Hronthar, no. But there are other telepathic species off-world that offer their services for a price. I've heard of an off-worlder I can hire to examine my mind."

She was still saying something, but Samir's attention was already drifting elsewhere.

It had been nearly eight hours since he'd last seen Warrehn. They'd had a hurried fuck after breakfast that didn't fully satisfy Samir, if he were honest. He'd orgasmed, obviously—for all his faults, Warrehn never left him physically unsatisfied—but Samir couldn't deny that the sex hadn't felt like enough. He'd simply gotten so used to prolonged physical contact during the tour that sleeping without Warrehn and not having access to him whenever he wanted made him hungry for more. A quick fuck with most of their clothes on just wasn't enough anymore.

He hadn't seen Warrehn since then. Warrehn had mentioned that he would be busy with Eridan that day, and it was pretty clear that he wanted to keep his precious baby brother away from the pure evil that was Dalatteya and Samir.

It was almost amusing—or would have been amusing if Samir didn't feel so frustrated. Although the concentration of the drug in his system had been gradually falling, he still needed to scratch the itch fairly frequently. Eight hours was pushing it.

Looking down at his communicator, he messaged Warrehn. *Are you busy?*

He counted to seventy-two before he received a response.

Working.

Samir scowled at the screen of his communicator. *Can't you take a break?*

He regretted the message as soon as he sent it. It sounded kind of… desperate and needy. Which he obviously wasn't. He was just frustrated. And he wanted to get off. He could jerk off, he supposed, but he didn't really feel like it. He wanted a hand on his cock, but only if that hand was Warrehn's. His large hand felt so amazing when Warrehn jerked him off as he fucked him.

A small noise left his mouth, and Samir flushed, hoping his mother hadn't heard it.

Unfortunately, his mother missed nothing. A frown was marring her beautiful features. "You're not even listening to me, Samir."

His communicator chimed, and Samir barely resisted the urge to look at it.

"Of course I'm listening, Mother," he said. "I just got distracted."

Her lips pursed, but thankfully, she didn't question him further and rose to her feet gracefully. "I will arrange a meeting with the foreign mind specialist," she said. "With any luck, they'll be able to remove the memory blocks and traps in my mind and I'll find out who did it."

Brushing her telepathic presence against Samir's in farewell, his mother glided out of the room.

Relieved to be alone, Samir dropped his gaze to his communicator and looked at Warrehn's response.

I'd like a break, but I can't exactly walk out on Councilor Hirosh. He is pissed enough as it is.

Samir caught his bottom lip between his teeth, hesitating. He shouldn't have felt sympathy toward Warrehn for having to put up with the insufferable old man. His mother would be pleased to learn that Warrehn was failing to find common ground with their nobles, all of whom had their own petty problems and demands.

But he wanted to see Warrehn—because of the drug. One unsatisfying quickie a day just wasn't enough.

Discarding his misgivings, Samir typed, *Councilor Hirosh has a feud with Councilor Zhang. Just say something uncomplimentary about Zhang, and he'll consider you his ally and will stop nagging you for no reason.*

There wasn't a reply for a long while.

Finally, his communicator chimed again. *Thanks.*

Samir found himself smiling. He could practically see the dark scowl on Warrehn's face, how much it pained him to thank him for anything.

Did it hurt? he sent.

Warrehn didn't reply.

Samir frowned, tapping on his knee in impatience. What an ass. Replying to messages was only polite.

At long last, his communicator chimed again.

Hirosh left. But I can't see you now—Eri is here.

Samir let out an aggravated groan. Eridan had the worst timing.

Your brother is no longer three, he typed. *He doesn't need you to hold his hand all the time.*

He's sulking over Idhron, Warrehn responded. *He needs me.*

I need you more. Samir typed it, but thankfully he had enough presence of mind to erase it before he could send it. Of course he didn't need *Warrehn.* He needed his cock. The fact that Warrehn was attached to it was of no import. There was basically no difference between Warrehn and a sex toy: both were just tools to satisfy him physically, nothing more.

So instead, Samir typed, *I can come, and you can leave your brother for a little while?*

It still seemed too desperate for his liking, but he couldn't not offer it. He missed feeling Warrehn with his *skin.* It was such a maddening feeling, but he yearned for it, for the sensation of Warrehn's firm, hard body against him, on top of him, inside of him, for his hands and mouth on him. He despised himself for needing it so viscerally, but that didn't change anything: his blood boiled with that need.

It felt like a small eternity passed before his communicator chimed again.

My brother doesn't know about our situation, and I don't want him to know.

Samir threw his communicator on the couch.

Fuck Warrehn. If he chose to spend his time with his little brother and didn't want Eridan to find out that they were fucking, Samir wasn't going to beg him.

He had his pride, damn it.

***

Unfortunately, by the evening, Samir's resolve had weakened.

He'd forgotten how bad it was, to feel so unfulfilled and unsatisfied, desperate for Warrehn's come inside him and unable to focus on anything else.

He didn't trust himself not to jump the asshole in front of his mother and Eridan, so he didn't join them for supper. He holed up in his rooms, put on his favorite relaxing music, and tried to think unsexy thoughts.

Spoiler alert: it didn't work.

He was still beyond horny, his thoughts having trouble focusing on anything but sex and Warrehn.

Samir had never hated himself more—and he'd never been angrier at Warrehn. So what if his precious little brother found out about their *situation*? Was Warrehn that ashamed of having sex with him? The answer was clearly yes.

And it pissed him off.

Apparently, being pissed off and very horny wasn't a good combination. That was how Samir ended up telling his personal assistant to find him a discreet escort for the night. Warrehn wouldn't fuck him? Fine. He could get another man to do it.

And never mind that the thought of sex with another man absolutely repelled him. It would be worrying if Samir wasn't sure it was the alien drug's doing. He could turn off the lights. He could trick his brain into believing that it was Warrehn. How hard was it to fool some alien drug?

"Any particular requests?" his PA, Tanita, said timidly.

She emanated surprise, and no wonder: Samir never used Calluvian escorts, due to NDAs being a headache. NDA-tech didn't work on telepaths.

Samir kind of wanted to ask for a well-endowed man, since his thoughts kept fixating on Warrehn's thick, veiny cock, but he still had some dignity left.

"None," he said, turning away. "Discretion is obviously of paramount importance. I'll be waiting in my rooms."

He had expected that he'd have to wait for half an hour at most—there were perks of being a royal—but an hour came and went.

Frowning, Samir was about to call Tanita when she called him herself.

"I'm sorry, Your Highness," she said. "But the escort I hired wasn't allowed into the palace."

"I beg your pardon?"

"It appears it was on His Majesty's orders."

Ending the call, Samir marched out of the room. His expression must have been thunderous, because the few servants he encountered shot him startled looks and hurried on their way.

He found Warrehn in the portrait gallery. He and his brother stood in front of the portrait of the former royal family: King Emyr with his golden-haired wife and two sons. Eridan looked uncannily like his mother, as similar to her as Samir was to his own. Warrehn didn't look much like his parents, though he had clearly inherited his height and build from his father. King Emyr's hair had been darker than Warrehn's, his blue eyes narrower and not as expressive. He had been as handsome as Warrehn, in a different way, but he emanated coldness that was obvious even in the picture. If Warrehn was fire and rage, the man in the portrait was ice and arrogance.

Not that Warrehn wasn't capable of being a high-handed, arrogant dick. He was *very much* capable of it.

"Care to explain yourself?" Samir said, stopping in front of Warrehn and glaring up at him. "Since when are my guests turned away without as much as asking me?"

"Your guests," Warrehn said flatly, crossing his arms over his chest, "have to pass the same security checks everyone else does. And that *guest* didn't pass them. He was unable to present a respectable reason for his visit."

"Bollocks!" Samir said, curling his hands into fists. "You can't control who I'm seeing—or what I'm doing with them."

"Do I need to remind you that this is *my* palace," Warrehn said. "Only I get to decide who enters it—or doesn't."

"You arrogant, controlling ass! Fine! I'll go to a hotel, then."

"You aren't going anywhere," Warrehn said, grabbing his arm.

"Unhand me," Samir said, shaking with a horrible mix of rage and need. It felt like the touch seared him. "You don't own me. What I do is none of your concern!"

"I'm the head of the Fifth Royal House," Warrehn bit off. "I pay for your bills, for your clothes, and for your *entertainment*. So you're very much my concern. Not to mention that the moment you check into the hotel, it'll be all over the gossip sites."

"Since when do you care about gossip?" Samir said, lifting his chin. It brought his mouth maddeningly close to Warrehn's, which didn't help his ability to think—or stay angry. Gods, he wanted to *bite* him, mold their lips together and kiss, and kiss, and kiss.

He wanted it so badly he was having trouble focusing.

Warrehn's eyes flicked down to his mouth, as if he were reading his thoughts. Samir licked his lips, and Warrehn's eyes became gratifyingly unfocused. *Kiss me. Kiss me. Put your tongue in me.* Samir was distantly aware that he was actively projecting those thoughts, but he couldn't bring himself to care. He wanted to be kissed. Wanted to feel this man with his skin, with his mouth, with his hands.

"Stop that," Warrehn said with a pinched, tight expression.

"I'm not doing anything," Samir said breathlessly, swaying toward him.

Warrehn caught him, pulling him flush against his body, and finally crushed their mouths together.

It was bliss, the sheer relief of it. Samir moaned, his arms snaking up around Warrehn's neck and his lips parting for his tongue. *Please.*

A cough barely penetrated through the fog of want and need in his mind. There was someone else there. He should probably care. He didn't. And thankfully, neither did Warrehn. He was kissing him with a force and hunger that rivaled his own, his large hands roaming all over his body, his cock pushing against Samir's stomach.

His cock. A fresh tremor of desire wracked his body as he thought of Warrehn's thick, long cock. Fuck, he wanted it, he wanted to touch it, to put it into his mouth and suck.

Warrehn made a growl of approval. As if in a dream, Samir dropped to his knees and greedily nuzzled the bulge under Warrehn's pants.

"Right," someone said awkwardly. "I'll go, then. Talk

to you later, Warrehn." There was the sound of retreating steps.

Noise. It was all just background noise. All Samir cared about was getting that cock in his mouth and worshiping it. His mouth was watering, his fingers trembling with impatience.

To his relief, Warrehn unzipped his fly and pulled his cock out, nudging it against Samir's lips. Moaning, Samir licked the leaking head before swallowing as much of the cock as he could. It didn't fit in his mouth, but Samir didn't care, sucking on it with relish, his eyelids dropping shut. Warrehn grabbed a fistful of his hair and *tugged*, sending tremors of pain and pleasure through his body.

"Fucking slag," he said, fucking into Samir's mouth steadily. "Were you gagging for cock so badly that you couldn't wait a little bit and hired a prostitute to give you a cock?" Thrust. "Whore."

The derogatory words shouldn't have made him feel more aroused. But they did. Fuck, they did. Being humiliated and treated like shit always aroused him, and Samir moaned around Warrehn's cock, reveling in the feeling of being used. He kind of wanted Warrehn to rough him up, slap him, for being a slag.

He felt a foreign surprise mixed with arousal, and realized that he must have projected his thoughts—or Warrehn was too strong a telepath not to pick them up.

"You *are* a slag," Warrehn said, grabbing his face with both hands and fucking into his mouth roughly, so deeply he was fucking his throat. "Look at you, on your knees in a public room anyone can enter, getting stuffed full of my cock and moaning like a slut. You want me to hit you? I can hit you." He slapped Samir across the face—not hard enough to truly hurt, but the sting was perfect.

Samir whimpered around the cock in his mouth, rubbing his own cock desperately.

Warrehn said softly, "Such a slut. If only people could see you now, their perfect Prince Samir getting his throat fucked like a ten-credit whore."

That was enough to send Samir over the edge. He came in his pants, and a moment later, his throat was flooded with Warrehn's come. He wanted it… he needed to taste it. He jerked himself off Warrehn's spasming cock and placed his lips over the head, sucking greedily, reveling in the taste and texture of the creamy seed filling his mouth.

Warrehn's grip in his hair turned into a caress, his fingers petting his scalp absentmindedly. Samir was this close to mewling. Everything felt toe-curlingly right. Perfect. Just as it should be.

The fingers in his hair went still.

"Fuck," Warrehn cursed, and, yanking his zipper shut, strode away.

Right.

Eridan.

He'd seen them.

***

"You don't owe me an explanation," Eridan said, his expression a mix of awkward, amused, and confused.

"I know I don't," Warrehn said. "But what you saw isn't—it isn't real. I don't like the guy and the feeling is mutual, I assure you."

Eridan raised his golden brows, conveying his skepticism without words. He looked so much like their mother when he did it that it made Warrehn feel more uncomfortable—and guiltier.

He was fucking the son of his mother's murderer. It was that bad. He wouldn't blame his brother for being disgusted. Sometimes he was disgusted with himself, too, no matter how much he might rationalize it. He was fucking the son of the woman who had killed his mother.

"You didn't exactly look like you didn't like each other," Eridan said dryly.

Warrehn sighed, running a hand over his face. "It's not real," he said, and then he explained what had happened.

By the time he was done, Eridan was frowning deeply.

He didn't speak for a while.

"I don't think it's Dalatteya's doing," he said at last. "She loves her son very much—I can sense her fierce love for him every time they're in the same room."

Warrehn couldn't deny it. He might not have been as strong an empath as his brother, but even he could tell that Dalatteya truly cared for Samir. It really didn't make any sense why she would put her beloved son into such a predicament.

"I'll look into it," Eridan said absently before his gaze trained on Warrehn again. "So the toxic possessiveness I just witnessed was the drug's doing, too?"

"Don't know what you're talking about," Warrehn said, looking away.

His brother snorted. "Please, War. You literally forbade his guest from entering the palace and then basically went all caveman on him: my palace, my rules, my territory!"

"I did no such thing," he said stiffly, rubbing the back of his neck. "But even if I did, it's the drug's doing."

"Right," Eridan said.

There was a great deal of skepticism in his voice, but thankfully he dropped the subject.

They spoke for a while, talking about what little Eridan remembered of their family. It wasn't much, and soon they lapsed into silence again—silence that was a little too awkward for Warrehn's liking. It frustrated him endlessly that his brother was still a stranger to him in a lot of ways. Twenty years apart would do that, and no matter how hard they both tried, the awkwardness lingered. It didn't help that part of Warrehn still resented Eridan's decision to return to the High Hronthar: he had accepted it, but it didn't mean he had to like it.

But it was his own fault. He wasn't good at being a big brother. Not only had he failed to make his little brother feel at home in their palace, but Eridan was now a witness to his inability to stay away from the son of their parents' murderer.

Warrehn grimaced. His attempt to stay away from Samir and spend time with Eridan had only made everything worse: he'd become so worked up that he had ended up kissing Samir in front of Eridan, like a green boy who couldn't help himself.

The memory of Samir's plush, eager lips sent a new wave of want through him, and Warrehn sighed inwardly. "I have to go."

Eridan gave him a long, assessing look, but thankfully didn't say anything.

Warrehn strode away.

Maybe it was for the best. Now that Eridan knew, he didn't have to hide his meetings with Samir. Why shouldn't he indulge himself for once?

For once?

You've done enough of indulging already.

Fucking Samir's mouth was the definition of self-indulgence. If Warrehn could blame his possessiveness on the alien drug and the mating instincts it caused, he didn't have an excuse for fucking Samir's mouth—or *kissing* him. Getting a blowjob wasn't exactly conducive to mating and procreating. Then again, fucking a man usually wasn't, either, but fucking Samir for real and coming in his ass made him feel such visceral relief and satisfaction Warrehn could only attribute it to the alien mating instincts.

Maybe that was why he didn't feel fully satisfied even after the blowjob. His body still ached with the urge to be balls deep in Samir, with the desire to take him. It was frankly disturbing how much he kept fixating on the concept of *taking* him. He wanted to take. And take. And take.

There was something heady about the way Samir gave himself to him, the way he was so pliant and eager for his touch, for his cock, for his mouth. Warrehn might hate what was done to them, but lately, when he was taking Samir, everything felt right—a feeling he'd rarely achieved ever since returning to Calluvia—and he craved the feeling, no matter how messed up it was. Nothing was fucking right about this situation, where consent was dubious at best. Warrehn knew that. But he couldn't change the way he seemed to have become addicted to the feeling. When he was touching Samir, the world *made sense.*

Once or twice, he had a disturbing thought that it was no longer the alien drug pushing him back into Samir's arms and willing body, but his own addiction. His own weakness.

No. He refused to believe that.

And yet here he was, standing in front of Samir's door, once again.

He glared at it, his throat working, as he tried to convince himself to walk away.

But before he could do it, the door opened, and there stood the bane of his existence, half-naked, plush lips bitten red and dark blue eyes fixed on Warrehn hungrily, burning with need.

Warrehn stepped inside the room.

The door clicked shut after him.

Chapter 15

Dalatteya didn't like lying to her son.

But unfortunately, she had no choice. If Samir ever found out the truth, he would think her insane.

The truth was, she had lied to Samir that she intended to go to an off-world telepath to have her mind examined. She had no intention of entrusting her mind to a stranger, a foreigner whose intentions she couldn't be sure of.

Not that she trusted the man she was about to see; not at all. But she could *control* him. And that made all the difference.

Dalatteya took a deep breath as she stopped in front of the gates before letting the scanner do its work. Only she and Uriel had access to this house—besides the droids that worked there.

As always, it took the scanner a while to finish scanning her retina, her DNA, and her fingerprints. At long last, the forcefield on the gates disappeared, allowing her to enter, and then immediately sealed the entire property. Some might consider such measures paranoid and excessive, but there could be no excess of paranoia when it came to *him*. He was smart. He was cunning. He was resourceful. He might escape. She could not—would not— allow him to escape.

Dalatteya entered the house and walked toward the library he was usually in at this hour.

It had been almost a month since her last visit. Both too long and not nearly long enough. She hated the way her heart was racing, like that of a young girl walking into the monster's lair. She loathed it. Utterly despised it. She knew with her mind that she was the one in control here, and yet…

"Are you going to stand there all evening?" The smooth, familiar voice made her insides quiver.

She walked into the library, her head held proudly. She wasn't going to show fear. She wasn't afraid. She was in control.

He was seated in the large chair by the fireplace, reading an old-fashioned paper book. He didn't lift his gaze from it as she entered the room, and she hated that he didn't. And she hated that she hated it. She hated a lot when she was around him.

He was the one who had taught her everything about hatred, after all.

"I was wondering when my jailer would finally grace me with her presence," he said, his gaze on the book. "Is it a gloating visit or are you just feeling horny, my dearest?"

Dalatteya glared at him, her eyes burning a hole in his face. It was dusted with dark stubble, tapering up to angular cheekbones. There wasn't even a hint of gray in his hair yet. He looked as fit and strong as a young man.

"I'm here because I had no other choice," she said coldly, her hands balling into fists behind her back. "It has been brought to my attention that there are memory blocks and mental traps in my mind. Is that your work?"

He finally lifted his gaze to her, his blue eyes unreadable.

"You flatter me," he said. "How would I accomplish such a thing when you have my telepathy bound and useless?" His eyes flickered to the psi-suppressors around his wrists, his lips twisting derisively. "I can't even meditate with those things, much less to do something so intricate as mind traps."

Dalatteya searched his face, but she couldn't find any sign of deception. Not that she would necessarily find anything; he was a better liar than she could ever hope to be. While what he was saying was supposed to be true, she couldn't be sure. He was a very strong telepath, the strongest she had ever known. She couldn't be sure that he hadn't found a way around the psi-suppressors.

"Then why didn't you say anything?" she said, walking over. "Don't tell me you haven't noticed them. Don't lie to me—I won't believe you."

A tiny smile curled his lips. "I have no intention of lying to you. I did notice that your mind has been tampered with. But why would a person tell anything to their jailer?"

She sneered. "Don't play the victim. It doesn't suit you. If you're jailed, it's because you're a monster that deserves nothing less. Besides, you can't argue that you're deprived of a person's freedom. You're not exactly a person, are you? The real Emyr was cremated twenty years ago. You're a *thing*. A thing *I* created. Just a clone I keep around because you have your uses."

The look he gave her was almost pitying as he leaned back in his chair and regarded her for a long moment. "You're nearly sixty years old, my darling. Entertaining foolish delusions doesn't suit a mature woman like yourself."

"I have no idea what you mean," she bit out. "And I'm not interested in listening."

Emyr—or rather, the man who wore Emyr's face—smiled. Dalatteya wanted to slap him, erase that infuriating smirk off those well-shaped lips.

Just a copy, she repeated to herself, trying to calm down. Emyr was dead. Dead. This was just a clone she had commissioned in secret, because she had needed to learn all the dirt Emyr had had on his lord-vassals, so she could keep them from trying to overthrow her and her son. That was the only reason this man existed.

"It's honestly adorable that you still keep clinging to the notion that you revived me for the sake of politics," false-Emyr said, his tone mild.

"I didn't revive you," she ground out. "Emyr is dead. You're just a clone, not a person. Clones don't have any rights in the Union of Planets. You breathe because *I'm* allowing you to. I'll dispose of you the moment you stop being useful."

Emyr laughed. "Do you actually believe what you're saying? I think it might be the funniest thing I've heard in years." He straightened up from his sprawl and put his hands on Dalatteya's waist. "You know that's a lie, my love."

Her stomach quivered. Gods, she hated his touch—hated how much she both craved it and hated it. "Stop calling me that," she snapped. "And yes, you're right: there was another reason why I cloned Emyr: death was too small a punishment for everything he's done. You—he killed my husband."

"Let me ask you a question," Emyr said, encircling Dalatteya's small waist with his long fingers. He pressed his thumbs against her belly and stroked it lightly. She had to swallow a whine threatening to leave her lips. Emyr was watching her reaction like a hawk as he continued.

"Instead of wasting highly illegal cloning resources on an evil monster like me, you could have used them on reviving your precious husband. Why didn't you?"

Dalatteya opened her mouth and closed it without saying anything, unable to speak. The thought hadn't even occurred to her.

Emyr smiled. "It's all right. I love you, too, darling."

"I don't *love* you," Dalatteya bit out, incensed. "If you were Emyr, you'd know that. I abhorred him—and I abhor you."

"You should make up your mind," Emyr said, still radiating amusement. "Either I'm not Emyr'ngh'zaver and I can't be responsible for anything he did to deserve your hatred, or I am. So what is it, Dalatteya?"

She glowered at him, hating the way he made her feel: foolish, illogical, and wrong-footed. Like a young, stupid girl.

His smile turning sardonic, he pulled her into his lap, her heaving breasts pressed against his firm chest. Her heart burned with hatred, and yet her nipples hardened into pebbles, aching for his touch, for his mouth. Her cunt pulsed with need.

Gods, she hated him, and she hated herself.

Her flesh might be weak, but she refused to give him the upper hand. She was in charge. She was in control, damn him.

Freeing herself from his grasp, Dalatteya got to her shaking feet and ordered, "Get on your knees."

His lips curling slightly, he did as he was told.

She hated that he looked in control even on his knees. His telepathy was bound and physically he was no threat to her, either—one word and the gravity restraints on his wrists would be enabled.

He should have looked powerless. Beaten. Humiliated.

He looked anything but.

Grabbing a fistful of his dark hair, Dalatteya pushed his face against her cunt, moaning as his mouth immediately found her hard clit through the thin fabric of her dress. He licked and sucked on her clit as his hands slowly lifted the hem of her dress. Cool air brushed against her legs, but she felt so hot she barely noticed the chill.

When his mouth finally touched her bare lips, she shuddered, pushing his face against her cunt tighter and tighter, choking him on her juices. She keened as he thrust his tongue inside her, fucking her with his tongue. So good. No other man had ever made her feel this good.

She whined when he suddenly stopped.

"Say my name," he said, his hot breath brushing against her aching clit.

"Get on with it."

Smiling, he *blew* on her clit. "Not before you say my name."

"I'm the one giving orders here," she ground out, yanking his face to her cunt again. "Lick."

He licked. He licked, sucked, and kissed her until she was sobbing from pleasure. She reached her peak fast—too fast—moaning something that was hopefully too unintelligible.

She was still panting when he broke the silence.

"You did say my name," he said, not without smugness.

"Shut up," she whispered, her fingers still buried in his hair. "I loathe you."

Emyr lifted his head from her cunt and licked his lips in a lewd manner.

"One would think you'd stop lying to yourself by now, darling. You didn't keep me alive for twenty years to use my knowledge of politics. You kept me alive because *you can't live without me.*"

She glared at him, breathing hard, and shoved him away in disgust. "You're delusional! You're nothing but a clone I keep around for my amusement."

Emyr laughed. "What is amusing is the way you still keep lying to yourself. A clone? I'm not a clone. I have all my memories intact, thanks to you. I simply inhabit a cloned body of *myself.* The fact that you bothered to clone my dead body and transferred my brain into it—which is highly illegal on all planets of the Union and would get you a life sentence if people were to find out—proves that you wanted *me* back. You wanted to look in *my* eyes, see *my* face, and have me remember you. All this effort and risk, just for a bit of revenge and help in politics? Stop lying to yourself, pet. You're smarter than that." Emyr looked her in the eyes. "But then again, you've always been excellent at lying to yourself. You even managed to convince yourself that I forced you. No one forced you into my bed, and no one forced you to enjoy being in it. But it's much easier to paint me as a monster when you have to explain to your son why you cheated on his father, right?"

"I said no every time," Dalatteya gritted out, glowering at him.

"Ah, yes," Emyr said with a sardonic smile. "It might have been convincing if I weren't a high-level telepath and couldn't read your thoughts and feelings. And they said *yes* and *please* every time."

"Shut up!" Dalatteya turned and all but ran out of the house, shaking with rage, guilt, and shame. No one could get under her skin like he did.

Gods, she hated him. How did he manage to still look like he owned the world, like he owned *her*, despite being bound and powerless? It should have been impossible.

What he should have been is dead, a voice said at the back of her mind as she strode through the garden. *He's not wrong. You brought Emyr back. You brought back the man who poisoned your marriage and made you unfaithful, the man who murdered your dearest friend. You brought back a monster, because—because you can't imagine your life without him.*

Dalatteya staggered to the bench, and wept, crying for the foolish young girl who had naively thought she'd ever be free of Emyr'ngh'zaver.

She would never be free of him.

There was the sound of footsteps, and then she felt familiar arms wrap around her.

Mentally exhausted, she laid her head on his wide shoulder, closed her eyes, and clung to him as he lifted her and carried her into the house.

***

Later, she lay in his arms, her body heavy with satiation. He was spooning her from behind, his softened cock nestled between her buttocks.

He kissed her on the neck and said, "I lied. I did put those protections in your mind."

She opened her eyes and stared at the wall. "How? You said—"

"The psi-suppressors do limit my telepathy. But you didn't take into account that I already have a pathway into your mind because of our natural compatibility and it's significantly easier for me to use my telepathy when I'm touching you. You serve as a conductor of sorts."

Dalatteya balled her hand into a fist. That cursed natural compatibility again. She had always both hated it and was grateful for it. She couldn't deny that their mental compatibility had made things easier for her back in her youth: were they not compatible, sex with Emyr would have been physically painful because of her childhood bond suppressing her ability to feel arousal. But her body had wanted Emyr, even back then. She had hated herself for it, hated her body for being unfaithful and welcoming Emyr's unwanted attentions, hated the ugly, unnaturally strong telepathic bond growing between them against her better judgment.

She had been right to hate it, it seemed.

"What did you do to me?" she said, her heart beating faster.

"Nothing bad. Mostly, the traps in your mind are aimed to prevent someone from learning about my continued existence. I did it to protect you." He nuzzled her hair, his large hand cradling her waist possessively. "I'm telling the truth, Latteya. I did it to protect you. What you did—what you're doing every day is a crime. Making a full clone of a royal is a very serious crime, since it puts in question the legitimacy of the line of succession."

She tensed in his arms. "You can't assume the throne. You're not Emyr in the eyes of the law. You're not a person."

"I am aware." His voice turned cold and hard. "You robbed me of my name, my throne, my power, and my freedom. If people find out about my existence, you will be in jail for the rest of your life and I will be eliminated as something that has no right to exist."

She turned onto her back. "Do you hate me?" she said, asking the question she hadn't asked in twenty years.

Emyr's gaze traveled over her naked form before returning to her eyes. "With every breath I take, my love."

"Don't call me that."

He leaned down and gave her a gentle kiss. "If I loved you less, I would have choked you with my bare hands," he said conversationally, rubbing his nose against hers. "But you know that, or you wouldn't have dared to sleep next to me."

Dalatteya didn't say anything to that. There was nothing to say. She tried not to think what it said about her that she felt perfectly safe sleeping in his arms. The arms of the man who had killed her husband. The arms of the man she had killed and who had every reason to hate her for that.

"Is that all you did to my mind?" she said, knowing better than to trust him.

Emyr nuzzled her cheek and didn't answer, the bastard.

Dalatteya frowned and opened her mouth to question him further, but he pushed his cock back into her, hard once again, and she sighed in delight, her thoughts scattering.

Nothing made her feel as full and perfect as he did.

And as wretched and disgusting.

Chapter 16

"My mother is acting strange."

Warrehn opened his eyes and looked down at the violet head resting on his chest.

As always, the sight brought mixed feelings. He knew he should put a stop to this. Kissing was bad enough. This was too much. He should tell Samir in no uncertain terms that his recently acquired tendency to cling to him after sex—to *cuddle*—was unwelcome.

Except the issue was… it wasn't unwelcome.

Over the course of the publicity tour, Warrehn had gotten used to them living on top of each other. Due to the security concerns, they hadn't stayed at hotels often— at least that was the official reason. Privately, Warrehn suspected Ayda just hadn't wanted to risk the hotel staff coming across them fucking, which, to be fair, wasn't a baseless concern.

In any case, Warrehn had been forced to share close quarters with Samir for nearly a month. It was natural that he'd eventually gotten used to Samir's scent being everywhere, used to touching him, and used to sleeping next to Samir or sprawled half on top of him after sex.

He wasn't sure at what point he'd stopped simply putting up with it and started liking it.

Even thinking about it made him uneasy, but he could no longer deny it. It was hard to remain in denial when he couldn't sleep alone anymore.

He had tried, just to prove to himself that he could, and he never slept well, his bed too empty and cold. He had felt like a kid unable to sleep without his favorite plush toy.

Obviously it was a habit caused by forced cohabitation. It should have gone away once they had arrived home. And maybe it would have gone away if he didn't continue to feed it by spending the nights with Samir more often than not. He had no excuse for that: the drug's effects had lessened enough that they didn't have to fuck at night. But still, he found himself reluctant to leave. Samir was warm and so very soft after sex, and he kept clinging to him, wanting cuddles, wanting kisses, wanting his touch, and it was—it was heady. It was addictive, to be wanted. To be needed.

Warrehn told himself that was all it was. It wasn't about *Samir* at all. It was just loneliness. As soon as the drug was out of his system, he'd find himself a lover, someone he could get physical touch and affection from. Someone who wasn't off-limits. Someone who wasn't a son of his enemy.

Speaking of the enemy…

"Strange?" Warrehn repeated. "What do you mean?"

"I'm not sure," Samir murmured, tracing the side of Warrehn's torso with his finger. "She's been weirder than normal. She disappears all the time somewhere and turns up looking thoughtful and distant."

"Probably plotting my death."

"It's not funny."

"I wasn't trying to be funny." Warrehn sighed. "Will you drop the pretense that your mother doesn't want me dead? It's just us here."

Samir folded his hands on Warrehn's chest and put

his chin on them. His dark blue eyes met Warrehn's, their expression open. "I have no idea what my mother is thinking or planning," he said quietly. "You may look into my mind if you don't believe me."

He looked so *sincere.* Warrehn stared at him at a loss, feeling his defenses crumble and suddenly wondering if it was Dalatteya's new tactic: to try to endear her son to him. As much as Warrehn hated to admit it, it was absolutely working. Samir looked so damn endearing and lovely with his pink, swollen lips and sultry eyes still glassy and soft after sex.

"That won't be necessary," Warrehn said stiffly. He couldn't risk delving into Samir's mind when they had such a strong natural compatibility. He had already noticed that they'd developed awareness of each other due to the prolonged exposure and physical touch. Mental intimacy was the last thing they needed, and it would only make a complicated situation disastrous. "What makes you think Dalatteya is acting strange?"

"She's my mother. I can sense it. And lately, she hasn't even asked about my health and the drug, which definitely isn't normal. It almost seems as though she doesn't care about it anymore and has her mind preoccupied with something else. It worries me."

Warrehn frowned, stroking Samir's lower back absently. "Can't you ask her what's wrong?"

"I have," Samir said, somehow managing to press closer to him. "She changed the subject and pretended she had no idea what I'm talking about. She's good at it." He put his head back on Warrehn's chest and sighed, radiating *comfy-good-secure.*

They were silent for a while before Samir murmured, "Is this freaking you out, too?"

He didn't need to clarify what he meant.

Warrehn exhaled audibly, not knowing what to say. He couldn't deny that it felt good to hold another person. Ever since his arrival to Calluvia, he had felt... lonely. He might have found his brother, but their relationship had never quite progressed to physical comfort before Eridan decided to return to the High Hronthar. Other than Eridan and Rohan—and the latter was too busy with his own clan's affairs—he didn't have anyone he trusted enough to drop his guard around, much less to hug. There had been Sirri briefly, but their relationship wasn't quite that of friends and definitely not the kind of friends that hugged.

So holding Samir and feeling his solid, warm body in his arms felt satisfying in ways Warrehn tried not to think about. He felt more content than he'd felt in... possibly ever.

"It's likely the drug," he said, staring at the ceiling blankly.

"Maybe," Samir said, nuzzling his chest. "Or maybe it's normal. I've never had a regular sex partner I could cuddle with, so I wouldn't know. The escorts I've hired on pleasure planets were obviously total strangers. I always felt so stressed that my preferences in bed would be leaked, so it wasn't exactly relaxing. The scandal would have been ugly if people found out that their future king hired prostitutes to degrade him and treat him roughly in bed."

Realizing he was holding Samir tighter than needed, Warrehn breathed deeply, fighting the vicious possessiveness, and forced himself to loosen his arms. He was the one in control, not the drug.

But it was also puzzling. He hadn't felt this possessive when Samir had told him that he'd had sex four times before him, and that had been less than a month ago.

Why was this shit getting worse?

"No," Samir said, squirming closer. "Do it again. Tighter."

Surprised, Warrehn slowly complied, tightening his arms again.

A small moan left Samir's lips. "Tighter."

Warrehn held him tighter, so tightly his grip was probably bruising, but Samir only radiated contentment, pleasure, and peace. Fuck, he felt perfect in his arms, and although Warrehn's cock was half-hard again, he didn't really feel any urgency to do anything about it. He didn't want to move.

"Has Eridan left, by the way?" Samir said sleepily, breaking the companionable silence.

"Yes, just a few hours ago. His *Master* came for him, and of course he went." Warrehn couldn't quite keep the bitterness out of his voice.

Samir nuzzled his chest, his lips brushing against Warrehn's nipple. "So the rumors are true? They're in a relationship?"

Warrehn opened his mouth but went still, realizing with a jolt that he had been about to tell Samir about his brother's forbidden relationship with the High Adept of the High Hronthar, his teacher. Fuck. When had he let his guard down so much?

"Yes," Warrehn said after a moment, figuring in the end that it was a good test of whether he could trust Samir a little. For all his faults, Idhron was fully capable of protecting Eridan if someone attempted to spread malicious rumors again—most of the press was in Idhron's pocket.

Samir hummed and went quiet for a while, tracing a finger over Warrehn's ribs absently. "You feel bitter and hurt about your brother leaving. And you blame yourself for your inability to keep him here. I can sense it so clearly when I'm touching you."

Stiffening, Warrehn said nothing.

Samir stroked his chest carefully, as if soothing an angry animal. "I think you shouldn't be so hard on yourself. If he chose to return to his old life, it doesn't mean he didn't like the life you offered. When you brought him here, he probably felt like his whole world was turned upside down. I know I did when I learned you were alive."

Frowning, Warrehn looked at him carefully. "That's different, though."

"Is it?" Samir said in a mild tone. "My mother raised me as a future king since I was a small child. I grew up with the knowledge that would be my life. When you came back…" He lifted his gaze and looked Warrehn in the eyes. "I felt like everything I knew about my life—about who I am—was a lie. I imagine your brother must have felt like that. Anchorless."

Warrehn had never thought of it this way. He studied Samir. "Do you still feel that way? Anchorless?"

Samir smiled crookedly. "In an amusing turn of events, I feel very much anchored right now. With your cock."

Warrehn's lips twitched.

"The world must be ending," Samir murmured with a smile, his thumb touching Warrehn's mouth.

Warrehn immediately stopped smiling.

"Nope, too late—I saw that!" Samir said, waggling his eyebrows. "The smile!"

Warrehn scowled, but even he could tell how unconvincing it was. He felt relaxed, amused even. Or maybe it was the orgasm. A good orgasm tended to do that to a man.

There was no other explanation for why he felt so comfortable holding Dalatteya's son like his favorite teddy bear and talking to him without animosity.

"I smile," Warrehn grunted.

"Not for real," Samir said, folding a hand under his chin so he could see Warrehn better. "I've seen you smile condescendingly, derisively, and in contempt, but never smile genuinely—until just now!" He tapped Warrehn's lips with his thumb, grinning. "It didn't hurt, see?"

Warrehn stared at his grinning face, at those pretty eyes sparkling with amusement and mirth.

He caught Samir's fingers in his hand and pushed them away from his mouth. "Stop flirting with me," he said roughly, his voice a stark contrast to the gentle way his hand couldn't seem to stop cradling Samir's fingers. "Stop being so..." He trailed off, unwilling to say it aloud. *Stop making me stare at you. Stop making me like you.*

Samir blinked and cocked his head to the side. "Being what?" he said, still smiling that maddeningly lovely smile.

Warrehn rolled them, pushing Samir under him. Samir gasped from the sudden movement and looked up at Warrehn breathlessly. "What—"

Warrehn pressed their foreheads together, his mouth dragging across Samir's smooth cheek. "I know you and your mother are up to something," he said against Samir's lips. "I know that. But..." He let out a frustrated sound and kissed him.

Samir parted his lips and kissed back, sucking on Warrehn's tongue eagerly. His shields were completely down, so Warrehn could feel all his surface emotions. He could feel that Samir could barely breathe under Warrehn's weight, but he loved it, loved being totally crushed under his body and surrounded by him.

Samir buried his fingers in Warrehn's hair and pulled him closer, tighter, until it felt like they were fused together. Somehow, it still wasn't enough. For either of them.

"Want you back in me," Samir said breathlessly.

Warrehn kissed him harder and gave him what they both wanted.

Chapter 17

Warrehn was dancing with Prince Aedan.

Samir stared at them across the ballroom, watching Prince Aedan smile up at Warrehn, his stupidly handsome face so close to Warrehn it was almost indecent. Aedan's eyes were flickering between Warrehn's blue eyes and his firm, stubbled jaw—or maybe he was looking at Warrehn's lips.

"They make a beautiful couple, do they not?"

Samir froze, darting his gaze to the side. There were two ladies just to his right, and they were also watching Warrehn and Aedan. He vaguely recalled that they were part of the Sixth Grand Clan. Prince Aedan's clan.

"Indeed they are," the other woman answered. "Just gorgeous."

Samir bit the inside of his cheek, returning his gaze back to the dancing couple. Gorgeous? He supposed the contrast between Warrehn's tall, muscular frame in all black and the graceful, elegant Prince Aedan in the pale colors of his House was striking. Their golden heads looked good together, although Aedan's hair was several shades lighter and much less splendid than Warrehn's. It wasn't even his natural hair color. Aedan was an empty-headed social butterfly concerned only with his looks and the latest fashion. What were they even talking about? The cut of Warrehn's jacket?

"I wonder if they'll get back together," the first woman said. "They were bondmates since they were toddlers. They must miss each other."

"Their bond was broken," Samir said, and realized too late that not only had he barged into someone else's conversation, but his voice had also come out too harsh.

The women were now staring at him oddly.

Forcing a smile, Samir tried to smooth over his blunder. "I don't think His Majesty is interested in restoring his childhood bond to Prince Aedan. They're now strangers to each other after decades apart."

"I don't know, Your Highness," the first woman said, looking back at the dance floor. "They certainly look very friendly now. Look how they're looking at each other."

Samir felt his jaw clench and had to make a conscious effort to look less tense. "If you'll excuse me," he said and strode away before he could say anything he would regret.

He left the ballroom and went into the gardens, not trusting his composure. He couldn't trust it, not when he felt like punching something, preferably Prince Aedan's ridiculously pretty face.

Fuck.

It was clearly the drug's side effect, but it didn't make it any easier.

He couldn't deny it: he was jealous. He was sizzling with jealousy and ugly possessiveness, wanting to shove Prince Aedan away and then latch himself onto Warrehn and *glue* them to each other, so that Warrehn couldn't dance with or look at or talk to anyone else.

"Get a goddamn grip," Samir said under his breath, raking a hand through his hair. He reached the quietest corner of the garden and sat down on the bench. He stared at the pond's surface, trying to meditate his anger and jealousy away.

It didn't work. He couldn't stop thinking about what Warrehn and Aedan might possibly be doing right now. Were they talking? Was Aedan making him smile? What if the women were right and Warrehn wanted Aedan back? And why wouldn't he? They *had* been bondmates. Prince Aedan was pretty, uncomplicated, and without any baggage. His mother hadn't murdered Warrehn's family, nor had she wanted to steal Warrehn's throne.

Samir chuckled harshly, as if his stomach wasn't churning with jealousy. "This is not real," he whispered, but although rationally he knew that this jealousy was caused by the drug, it didn't change anything. He burned with jealousy.

"Samir?"

He whipped his head around and exhaled when he saw Warrehn standing there. He ran his eyes over Warrehn's tall body, searching for any sign of rumpled clothes. But Warrehn's clothes were impeccable. He'd even thrown his heavy black mantle over his shoulders. He looked so handsome Samir's mouth literally watered.

"Come here," Samir heard himself say.

Warrehn lifted his eyebrows but walked closer and sat down beside him.

Samir knew he shouldn't. They were at a ball, in someone else's house, and he had no idea if there were cameras in the garden. But he couldn't help himself. He wanted to kiss him and touch him so badly he was shaking with it.

He straddled Warrehn's lap and kissed him needily. His, his, his. He was here, with him, not with Aedan.

Warrehn tried to break the kiss. "Wait—Samir—we can't do it here—" He didn't sound very convincing, considering that he was kissing him back, his arm tight around him. "We should stop."

"No," Samir said, cradling his stubbled cheeks with his hands and kissing him deeper. He felt like he could swallow him, swallow this man and keep him inside him forever.

"We can't have sex here," Warrehn said, kissing his chin, and then his neck, his mouth hot and perfect.

Don't need sex, Samir thought, his eyes closing in bliss. *Just keep touching me.*

There was a distant feeling of alarm at the back of his mind, but it quickly faded when Warrehn's mouth reclaimed his lips. Mmm… So good.

"Have you lost your senses?!"

They broke the kiss at the sound of the familiar voice.

Still breathless and flushed, Samir focused his gaze on Warrehn's publicist and gave her a sheepish look.

Ayda glared at him, looking entirely unimpressed. "Your Highness," she ground out, her hands on her hips. "Please get off His Majesty's lap." When he reluctantly complied, she said, "Good. Now go back to the ballroom and stay on the opposite side of the room from the king."

Samir looked at Warrehn.

Warrehn looked back at him, his eyes glinting hungrily, his long, powerful body rigid with tension.

"For crying out loud," Ayda said. "You're forbidden from looking at each other, as well." Huffing, she took Samir's arm and all but dragged him toward the ballroom. "I don't get paid enough for this, damn it."

"We're not that bad," Samir said defensively.

He shut up when Ayda shot him an incredulous look.

All right, maybe she had a point.

***

"His Majesty is unavailable, Your Highness."

Samir frowned at Warrehn's secretary and looked at the closed door that led to Warrehn's office. "Even for the royal family?"

The man hesitated. "Do you have a prior appointment, Your Highness? His Majesty told me not to disturb him. He has work that needs to be finished soon and he doesn't want any distractions. I'm really sorry."

His tone was very final, and in any other circumstances, Samir would have turned around and left, but…

He needed to see Warrehn—that is, he needed Warrehn's *opinion* on the education bill he wanted to push in the next session of their clan's council. If Warrehn didn't support it, all his efforts would be largely in vain. He might be the heir to the throne currently, but people knew it was a temporary situation at best, and as soon as Warrehn got a real heir, Samir would become irrelevant, since Warrehn's consort would be voting as the regent until the heir turned twenty-five.

Samir pursed his lips, trying to banish the image of Prince Aedan from his head.

"It's kind of urgent," he said. "Don't worry, I'll tell him you tried to stop me." And with that, he marched toward the door.

"Your Highness—"

Samir entered the office and shut the door.

Warrehn lifted his gaze from the holo-document in front of him, something flickering in his eyes when he saw Samir. "I'm busy now, Samir," he said.

Clearing his throat a little, Samir smiled sheepishly and retrieved a datapad out of his pocket. "I'm here for this. An educational reform I've been planning for a while."

Warrehn didn't even glance at it, his gaze intent on Samir's face.

"What?" Samir said with a crooked smile. "This is important, really."

Warrehn shook his head, leaning back in his seat. It should have been outlawed, the way he looked so mouthwateringly good with that blue dress shirt hugging his broad shoulders and thick biceps. It brought out his eyes and looked wonderful against his bronzed skin. Samir swallowed as Warrehn loosened his cravat, his long fingers working on it unhurriedly as his blue eyes remained on Samir.

"Do you want me to support it?" Warrehn said.

Samir cleared his throat a little. "That would be the desirable outcome, yes."

Warrehn got to his feet and walked over. Taking the datapad from Samir's hand, he set it on the desk behind him.

Samir wet his dry lips.

Warrehn looked at him. Just looked.

And fuck it, Samir couldn't stand it anymore. He took a step closer and nudged his nose against Warrehn's, shivering as he breathed in his familiar, nice scent. "Hi," he said, looping his arms around Warrehn's neck and smiling helplessly.

"I do have a country to run, you know," Warrehn said, but his arms wrapped around Samir and held him tightly just the way Samir liked it, making him feel wonderfully grounded and safe and emptying his head of all thoughts.

Sighing happily, Samir hugged him back and tilted his face up, wanting kisses.

"Samir," Warrehn said hoarsely, trailing hot, open-mouthed kisses all over his face before finally claiming his mouth.

Samir couldn't breathe. He felt like he could expire from pleasure and delight, his hands roaming all over Warrehn's strong back as he sucked on Warrehn's tongue with ravenous little moans. Very distantly, at the back of his mind, he was appalled and embarrassed by his own behavior—he was here on business, not for this; really—but he couldn't stop, couldn't stop kissing Warrehn and touching him and wanting him. He wanted to *consume* him whole.

He shoved Warrehn onto his desk, straddled him, and yanked Warrehn's fly open.

***

Samir had never imagined that he would be insane enough to have sex in the throne room.

But apparently, he was.

He let out a long moan as he slowly lifted himself off Warrehn's thick cock and dropped back onto it hard. He cried out, and then buried his face in Warrehn's shoulder, trying to unsuccessfully muffle his noises.

Warrehn's fingers had a bruising grip on his ass as he guided Samir and helped him ride his cock. "Quiet," he said, his voice tight, almost pained. "The throne room doesn't have a lock."

Samir was well aware of that. Anyone could enter and find him riding the king's cock. The humiliating thought sent a wave of arousal straight to his cock.

Warrehn chuckled, fucking up into him. "You kinky little shit," he said gently, breathing heavily against the side of his face. "You like it—that people might enter the room and see you on my cock, servicing your king."

Samir whined, moving his hips faster and faster, the slap of his bare thighs against Warrehn's pants obscenely loud. Warrehn was fully clothed while he was naked from the waist down. If anyone were to enter, they would see his naked ass first, and then Warrehn's thick, red cock moving in it rhythmically. Samir groaned, imagining people's open-mouthed stares, how shocked and appalled they would be.

"Kiss me," he begged, panting.

Warrehn kissed him, his strong hand cradling his nape gently.

When they both finished, Samir laid his head on Warrehn's wide shoulder and closed his eyes, feeling so amazing he felt like purring.

Warrehn chuckled, wrapping his mantle around him. "Don't fall asleep on me. Not here."

"Mmm," Samir said, nuzzling his muscular neck. "Let's go to your room, then. We can sleep there."

"I can't," Warrehn said with a sigh. "I have a mountain of paperwork in my office I need to deal with first. You can take a nap in my room while you wait for me."

Samir thought about taking a nap. It did sound appealing. But...

"I'll help you," Samir said, squirming closer to Warrehn. "I'm good at paperwork."

"All right," Warrehn said after a moment. "Let's go."

Samir smiled.

Chapter 18

"Where have you been?"

Samir froze as he entered his rooms, looking at his mother seated on his couch.

Her blue eyes flicked all over him, her lips pursing in obvious distaste.

Samir flushed, suddenly very self-conscious about his half-dressed state and unkempt hair. He hoped there weren't new hickeys on his neck. He usually used a dermal regenerator, but he hadn't exactly expected his mother to be waiting for him in his room in the middle of the night.

"It's three in the morning," Dalatteya said.

Samir crossed his arms over his chest and nodded. "Indeed, Mother. Which makes me wonder why you're still up at this hour."

Fixing him with a flat look, she got to her feet. "I've had enough, Samir. I stayed silent about the situation, because I felt guilty about my part in it, but that is enough. It's been nearly two months! Dr. Jihan said your—your symptoms were supposed to have been completely gone by now. Instead, I find you absent from your rooms at three in the morning, and don't you dare lie to me that you weren't with that man! I can sense his telepathic mark all over you."

Samir held his mother's gaze with some difficulty.

"I'm handling the situation as best I can," he said, very evenly. "Need I remind you that I wouldn't be in this situation if it weren't for you?"

"I already said I was sorry," Dalatteya said, stepping closer and laying her hands on his shoulders. "Darling, look at me."

"I'm looking at you, Mother," Samir said, looking down at her.

"Look me in the eye and tell me you don't want that man."

Samir let out a laugh. "Mother, you know very well that I can't really say that with the alien drug in my system—"

"I authorized Dr. Jihan to use our palace AI to run a scanner on you. He said there's approximately 0.002% of the drug left in your system. You're effectively back to normal."

Samir opened his mouth and closed it without any sound leaving it.

His first urge was to say that it must have been a mistake, that of course it was a mistake, that it couldn't possibly be true. But then he thought about how clear his recollection of sex had been lately. He thought about how he hadn't thought of Warrehn in terms of "breeder" and "mate" in a long time. He thought about the fact that lately he fixated more on Warrehn's kisses and Warrehn's arms around him than on the sex. He even enjoyed doing Warrehn's *paperwork* with him, for fuck's sake.

Samir's stomach dropped.

"Now look me in the eye and tell me you don't want that man."

He wet his lips with his tongue. "Why does it matter, Mother? Sex is just sex. Don't tell me you've never enjoyed sex with someone you didn't like."

The look Dalatteya gave him was positively chilling.

"Don't play stupid, Samir. Are you claiming you don't like him? I've seen the way you look at him: like a besotted, foolish boy. You have lost sight of the goal—which is removing Warrehn from the picture."

Samir's heart started beating faster. "Mother, I don't think—"

"That is your problem, Samir: you don't think! The longer Emyr's spawn stays on the throne, the more used to him our people will become. His association with you in public already made him more popular than he has any right to be. We can't wait any longer if we want him removed from the throne—"

"I don't want it," Samir said quietly.

"I beg your pardon?"

Samir forced himself to look her in the eyes. "I never wanted it. It was your dream to see me on the throne, not mine. I did it to make you happy, Mother. But now I'm done. Stop plotting against Warrehn, stop scheming. He's a perfectly good king. I don't want his throne."

He tried to ignore the disappointment on her face. He was a grown man. He didn't need his mother's approval.

"It's not just about getting the throne back, Samir," she said, her voice toneless. "He's been investigating the past, looking for proof of me killing his parents and attempting to murder him and his brother. It's only a matter of time until he finds something and gets me arrested."

Samir's heart skipped a beat.

His mother smiled sadly. "Is the infatuation you feel for that man more important for you than me?"

Samir swallowed. "Mother—"

"End it, Samir. Now. Put distance between you. If you aren't going to help me, at least don't get in the way."

And with that, she left, her heels clicking loudly.

Samir shut the door and sagged back against it, looking blankly at the opposite wall.

***

He didn't get a wink of sleep that night.

Come morning, he felt barely functional—and still without any clue what to do. He loved his mother, he felt fiercely protective of her, but… But.

Samir was just finishing getting dressed when there was a sharp knock on the door.

His eyes widened, his heart beating faster.

"Hey," Warrehn said when he opened the door, stepping forward and laying his hands on Samir's hips in a such a casually proprietary manner Samir did a double-take and blushed, confused and flustered. He didn't understand. If they really were back to normal, why was Warrehn still behaving like this? Or could Warrehn still be affected? Samir did recall Dr. Jihan saying that there was more of the drug in Warrehn's system than his, but…

Warrehn pulled him close, moving him easily with a firm pressure on his hips. Samir could have resisted.

He didn't.

"Hey," he said with a weak smile.

Warrehn frowned, his blue eyes flicking over him. "Everything all right? You're trembling."

"It's just chilly here," Samir said. "Temperature controls must be malfunctioning."

"Hm," Warrehn said, his gaze becoming heavy-lidded. Leaning in, he nuzzled his ear and bit his earlobe lightly. "I can warm you."

Samir inhaled shakily, his mind becoming slow and

foggy. He smelled so good. "I…" he said. "Warrehn, we need to—"

Warrehn kissed him, his strong arms pulling him flush against him. And Samir's thoughts scattered. A small whine rose up in his throat, and he kissed back hard, feeling ravenous and desperate in ways he'd never felt before. He *would* tell Warrehn that the drug was out of their systems—just a little bit later. Some more kissing wouldn't hurt anyone, right?

Right?

Much later, Samir was staring at the ceiling blankly, still panting after his orgasm, pinned under Warrehn's larger body, Warrehn's cock softening in him.

"I'll move," Warrehn said into his neck, his voice still sounding a little wrecked. "I'm too heavy."

Samir grabbed his shoulders when he attempted to pull away. "No," he said, wrapping his limbs around Warrehn as tightly as he could. "Don't. Please." *Stay in me.*

"You're weird today," Warrehn said, but he complied, sucking a bruise on Samir's neck lazily.

On any other day Samir would have protested—he hated being forced to use dermal regenerators all the time—but the words got stuck in his throat now.

He wanted those bruises now. Something to remember this by. As soon he told Warrehn that they were back to normal, this would stop. There would be no more kisses, no more late-night conversations in bed, no more of this intimacy and warmth. Warrehn would go back to hating him and his mother, even more so if Samir suddenly started giving him the cold shoulder, as his mother wanted. Either way, this was… pointless. Hopeless.

There would always be a gulf between them. There was no real choice for Samir.

He couldn't allow his mother to be arrested; he wouldn't be able to live with himself. But he couldn't imagine letting his mother hurt this man, either. There was no acceptable solution. It was a lose-lose situation.

A crushing wave of despair swept over him, making it hard to breathe.

Warrehn stopped sucking on his neck and lifted his head. "Samir?" he said, his eyes looking at him searchingly.

Fuck. He'd forgotten what a strong telepath Warrehn was. He must have projected some of his thoughts and emotions.

Samir forced another weak smile. It was fine. He was fine. It wasn't as though he had serious feelings for Warrehn. Of course he didn't. He didn't. He had just gotten… a little infatuated. A little too used to him. To his touch. To his scent. To the feeling of utter safety and contentment with the world while in his arms.

"I… Can you stay for a while? I know you have a meeting with the councilors soon, but…" He trailed off, despising himself for his inability to rip the bandage off and be done with it. "I just feel down, I guess. You know how sometimes you wake up already in a bad mood, anxious about something you can't put a finger on?"

Warrehn nodded, settling his weight back on top of him. It made breathing significantly more difficult, but Samir didn't mind, relishing how wonderfully solid, firm, and grounding he was. The cock in him started hardening again, and Samir smiled, kissing Warrehn's shoulder. "Another round?" he said eagerly.

"Aren't you sore?" Warrehn said, looking at him with a slightly puzzled expression.

He was. He didn't care. He wanted to feel this for days.

"No," Samir said, burying his fingers in Warrehn's thick hair, hating how needy he felt. "Kiss me."

Warrehn did, and the rest of the world faded away. There was only Warrehn's warm, sensual lips, and his powerful body moving on top of him, inside of him. It felt achingly perfect.

"Deeper," Samir asked, digging his fingernails into his back. "Want you deeper."

Warrehn gave it to him deeper, but no matter how good it felt, Samir didn't feel him deep enough.

He came with a frustrated cry, his eyes wet and his heart aching.

Chapter 19

Rohan wasn't a huge fan of balls. He would rather spend the evening at home with his bondmate and little daughter, but unfortunately, they did have to make public appearances once in a while. And this evening was one of those occasions. On the bright side, he got to see his best friend at social functions like this, which was pretty rare these days, due to both of them being very busy with their respective countries' affairs and families.

Though it probably wasn't accurate to call Warrehn's so-called relatives *family*, not with the way Warrehn was looking at Prince Samir across the ballroom.

"You should try to be less obvious, War," Rohan murmured.

Warrehn made a noncommittal noise, his gaze flicking back to Prince Samir. Rohan wasn't even sure he'd heard him.

"I thought the drug would have been out of your system by now," Rohan said, keeping his expression neutral. There were always eyes on them, and he couldn't afford to look concerned.

Warrehn *shrugged*.

This time Rohan struggled to keep his expression blank. It was very unlike Warrehn to be so noncommittal and careless about a situation he hated.

Disconcerted, Rohan followed Warrehn's gaze to Prince Samir.

The prince certainly was beautiful. He was almost as gorgeous as Jamil, and that was the highest praise a man could receive for his looks—or a woman, for that matter. Objectively, Rohan could see the appeal, but it was very unlike Warrehn to let his cock do the thinking. Warrehn *hated* Dalatteya. Utterly loathed her. Rohan had thought that would be enough to make Dalatteya's son as loathsome in Warrehn's eyes.

Perhaps he had thought wrong.

"If you don't quit looking at him like you want to eat him, people will notice," Rohan said.

Warrehn flinched and looked away, scowling. That expression was much more familiar, but it failed to ease Rohan's concern, considering that Warrehn's gaze almost immediately returned to Samir, as if… as if he couldn't help himself.

Fucking hell.

Now he was more than just concerned. He was very much alarmed.

"I'm simply observing him," Warrehn said, his voice as stiff as his posture. "He's acting odd."

Rohan decided to humor him. "In what way?"

"He's been off for a few days. He spaces out often, and when he realizes that I've noticed, his telepathic presence gives off guilt and misery."

"That's it?" Rohan said.

Warrehn looked back at Samir, loosening his cravat. "No," he said in a clipped voice. "When he isn't distant, he's been kind of—needy."

"In what way?"

Warrehn didn't answer for a while.

At last, he said, without looking at Rohan, "He wants to be held. He spends every night in my bed and gets awfully clingy in the morning, not letting me leave. I had to cancel multiple morning meetings lately."

Rohan eyed his friend curiously. "Had to? You don't have to indulge him, you know."

A muscle twitched in Warrehn's jaw. "You don't understand," he said. "The drug is—it's impossible to resist. It's…" He trailed off, his shoulders tensing and his expression darkening.

Rohan followed his gaze.

Prince Samir was speaking to his mother. Although both of them had polite smiles on their faces, even Rohan could tell that something about the interaction was off. They seemed to be arguing, with Dalatteya speaking fast, and Samir's body language getting defensive.

Rohan turned to Warrehn, but his friend was already moving toward the pair.

Curious, Rohan followed him. He hadn't really seen Warrehn interact with Dalatteya and her son since the drug debacle had started. He hoped Warrehn wasn't about to make a scene.

He struggled to catch up to Warrehn: he didn't have Warrehn's ridiculous shoulders to push his way through the crowd, nor his unfriendly scowl to deter people from speaking to him. When he finally caught up to his friend, Warrehn had already reached Dalatteya and her son.

"Is something wrong?" Warrehn said.

Rohan couldn't see his face from this angle, but he could see Samir's and Dalatteya's. The woman stiffened, her expression becoming more closed off. Samir's body language was a study in contradictions: the tension in his shoulders eased and his body swayed toward Warrehn at first, before he glanced at his mother and seemed to become more anxious.

"Everything is absolutely fine," Dalatteya said with a beautiful smile. "I was just discussing with Samir how wonderful it is that you're back to your normal selves. I'm sure you were delighted when Samir informed you of that days ago. Weren't you? Your Majesty."

Warrehn's body became absolutely rigid. He didn't say anything for a moment, his head turning to Samir, who flushed, projecting misery and anxiety.

"What is she talking about?" Warrehn said, his voice flat but full of tension. "Samir."

Rohan cocked his head to the side, curious. It was extremely unlikely that Warrehn somehow hadn't understood what Dalatteya had said. Knowing his friend, Rohan had expected him to explode at Dalatteya's words, not to be patient enough to ask Prince Samir for clarification. Judging by the frown on Dalatteya's face, she had expected the same. Warrehn's composure, no matter how feigned it was, was really surprising. Warrehn hated being lied to. The fact that Prince Samir hadn't told him that the alien substance was out of their systems should have made him angry enough to lose his composure in public—which was probably Dalatteya's aim, come to think of it.

Prince Samir stepped closer to Warrehn and made an aborted move, as if he intended to touch his hand. "I can explain," he said, looking Warrehn in the eyes beseechingly. "Please let me explain."

Warrehn's throat bobbed, his telepathic presence exuding anger, disbelief, and confusion. He looked like he'd been hit with a truck, as if he had hoped Samir would say that Dalatteya was lying.

With a pained grimace, Samir glanced around and then smiled. "People are watching. You should smile."

"I don't really feel like smiling right now," Warrehn said, but to Rohan's astonishment, he forced a faint, twisted smile onto his lips. His body was still stiff with tension and suppressed anger, but he *was* smiling.

Rohan looked at Prince Samir with new eyes, not sure whether to be pleased or alarmed. He'd always wished for his friend to meet someone who would soften his rough edges and serve as a calming influence for him, but he didn't think that person should be Dalatteya's son.

Prince Samir smiled wider at Warrehn and carefully laid his hand on Warrehn's elbow. "Come. Walk with me."

"Samir," Dalatteya said sharply, but her son ignored her and led Warrehn out to the nearest balcony, leaving people staring after them and whispering in their wake.

***

"Out," Warrehn said flatly, and the three young men conversing on the balcony scrambled to comply, muttering *Your Majesty* under their breaths.

It would be amusing if it weren't so exasperating—and if Samir didn't have more important things to worry about.

"Did you have to be that rude?" Samir chided softly as the balcony doors closed after the young men. "They'll gossip."

Warrehn crossed his arms over his chest and leaned back against the door, his handsome face hard and unforgiving. "I don't care. Explain yourself."

Samir stepped closer and put his hand on Warrehn's chest. "War—"

"Don't," Warrehn said, a muscle flexing in his jaw. "Don't touch me."

It shouldn't have hurt. It shouldn't have made his chest feel hollow and achy.

"Stop that," Warrehn ground out, looking at him with a tight, sour expression. "You have no right to look that way—so hurt—it makes me—" He cut himself off, radiating frustration with every line of his tall body.

Biting his lip, Samir wrapped his arms around himself. "Mother told me that the drug was gone from my system a few days ago," he said quietly. "I did intend to tell you, I truly did. But I…" He trailed off, his face becoming warm.

"You what?"

Screw it.

Samir stepped forward and looped his arms around Warrehn's waist, ignoring his hostile glare.

"I said don't touch me," Warrehn gritted out, his gaze a mix of fury and endearing confusion.

Samir wanted to kiss him, badly.

He didn't. Instead, he put his head under Warrehn's chin and hugged him harder, ignoring Warrehn's attempts to dislodge him. It was nothing like their usual cuddles in bed—it was like hugging an unresponsive statue—but it still brought him some comfort, feeling Warrehn's firm body against him and smelling his scent.

"Stop this," Warrehn said tersely. "Stop doing this and explain yourself."

"This is me explaining myself," Samir said into Warrehn's neck. "I couldn't give this up. You made me addicted to this, so this is all your fault."

Warrehn gave a harsh chuckle. "You can't seriously expect me to believe this lousy explanation."

"You'll have to, because it's the only one you're going to get. I don't have another. This is the truth."

"I don't believe you," Warrehn said, but his body was no longer as stiff and unwelcoming as it had been.

Samir rubbed his nose against Warrehn's throat. "You're welcome to read my mind if you don't believe me."

"Memories and thoughts can be forged," Warrehn said.

Samir lifted his head. "Not in a merge. I've heard you can't lie in a merge."

A deep wrinkle appeared between Warrehn's brows. "No," he said curtly, his tone final. "I'm not doing that." Despite his harsh tone, his body relaxed further against Samir's, his hands coming to rest on Samir's lower back.

"Why?" Samir said with a small smile. "Because it's too intimate?"

"Because telepathic merges are illegal," Warrehn said. "I wouldn't put it past your mother to accuse me of illegally merging with you to get me arrested and declared unsuitable to rule."

Samir blinked. "I hadn't even thought of it," he said, a little surprised that such a scheme had occurred to Warrehn first. "I'm not conspiring with my mother, Warrehn. If I were, why would she expose that the drug is gone from our systems, making me look like a liar? She's worried I have gotten attached to you."

Warrehn gave him a long look, his gaze unreadable.

"Are you claiming that you are?" he said in a clipped voice. "Attached."

Samir bit the inside of his cheek, gathering up his courage.

He whispered, "Are you claiming that you aren't?" He looked pointedly at the lack of space between them, at Warrehn's arms around him, before meeting Warrehn's gaze. "The last few days, it wasn't the drug, Warrehn. It was us. You and me. Nothing else."

Warrehn's throat worked. His hands on Samir's lower back flexed. "I don't—I *can't* trust you."

Samir felt a crushing wave of sadness. His eyes were suddenly burning.

This was hopeless. He'd always known how hopeless this thing between them was, but it hit him differently now. They could never be anything, no matter how good—how right—being in Warrehn's arms felt. Lack of trust would make any relationship between them impossible, regardless of their feelings.

He couldn't even blame Warrehn for not trusting him; he wouldn't trust himself if their situations were reversed, either. His mother *had* killed Warrehn's parents and wanted to remove him from the throne and Samir wasn't going to do anything to help Warrehn prove her guilt.

"I understand," Samir said, trying to swallow the painful lump in his throat.

They looked at each other for a long moment, and Samir suddenly realized that this was goodbye. This was the last time they would stand like this, touch like this. They could have been something special, something great, if they weren't the people they were. Maybe in another life, they would have been.

His eyes stinging, Samir kissed Warrehn on his stubbled cheek, his eyelids dropping shut as he inhaled deeply.

"Be safe," he whispered, his throat aching.

Warrehn's arms squeezed around his ribs to the point of near-pain. It hurt in ways that had nothing to do with the physical pain.

And then Warrehn let go. Without looking at Samir, he opened the door and left.

Chapter 20

When Samir returned to the ballroom, Warrehn was already gone. It was probably a good thing; they'd already supplied enough fodder for gossip as it was. Samir held his head high as he approached his mother. Dalatteya was too socially conscious to glare at him openly, but he could feel her anger through their familial bond. Samir tucked her hand into his elbow and led her out of the ballroom.

They were silent on the way home.

They were silent until they reached Samir's office.

As soon as the door slid shut after them, Dalatteya exploded. "What were you thinking? Do you have any idea how bad it looked when you strolled out of the ballroom with that man and then stayed alone with him on the balcony after he had kicked out the other guests there? If I weren't there, your reputation would be in tatters!"

Samir found it hard to care.

He sat down in his chair behind the desk and looked at his mother tiredly. "Why did you do it? I would have told him the truth myself."

"When?" Dalatteya sneered. "I'm not blind, Samir. I've seen the way you look at him. It has become clear to me that you were getting unacceptably infatuated with that man. Something had to be done about it. I did what I had to. It's for your own good."

Samir closed his eyes for a moment before opening them and saying in a measured, flat voice, "Congratulations. You accomplished what you wanted. Warrehn and I are done." He held her gaze. "Now listen to me, Mother. I know I can't stop you from scheming and trying to remove Warrehn from the throne. But if you harm him physically, if you arrange his death, I will *never* forgive you. And if you do something else to him to get him off the throne, I will abdicate. So leave him alone."

His mother stared at him.

"Oh, my darling," she whispered at last, walking over and hugging Samir's stiff body to her chest. She sighed, sadness filling their familial bond. "I should have had that man killed the moment he returned. He isn't worth it, sweetheart. Men of that family are poison." Her voice cracked. "You deserve better, believe me."

Samir's eyes burned. He let the tears fall, letting them soak his mother's dress. He hated it, hated the unfairness of it, hated that even now, he couldn't hate her. She was his mother. He knew that everything his mother had done was out of—sometimes misguided—love for him. Well, that and her hatred for King Emyr.

"He isn't his father," he whispered.

Dalatteya's arms around him stiffened. "Perhaps," she conceded after a moment. "But he's his father's son. And he will never forget it. He despises us and wants his revenge. That would never change. The—the attraction between you will fade in time, and there will be only hatred, mistrust, and resentment left. You deserve better, my darling." Her voice became wistful. "You deserve love that isn't toxic. Love that knows no hatred. I want that for you."

"Because that's what you had with Father?"

His mother took a moment to reply. "Your father and I shared deep affection for each other. We grew up with our minds intimately connected ever since we were toddlers. We didn't know what it meant not to love each other. But even our relationship was soon poisoned by the anger and resentment caused by my involvement with the king."

Samir frowned. "Surely Father didn't blame you for the king's sick interest in you?"

His mother cleared her throat a little. "It was—complicated. My point is, I wish for you to have the kind of love I've never had: love without toxicity. Love that brings you happiness." She threaded her fingers through Samir's hair. "In fact, I think it's about time we find it."

Samir pulled back from her embrace and looked at her. "What?"

Dalatteya smiled, her eyes lighting up. She clapped her hands in excitement. "Yes, what a marvelous idea! Why didn't I think of it before? In my defense, we were so busy preparing for your coronation that finding you a good match was pretty low on my list of priorities, but all things considered, there's no better time than the present! We shall announce that you're looking for a spouse tomorrow, and I'm sure we will have an abundance of widowed or bondmateless suitors—perhaps even off-world politicians—"

"Mother, wait!" Samir said faintly, his gut churning with unease. "I don't want a spouse—"

"Nonsense," Dalatteya brushed him off, her eyes glinting madly in a way that indicated that she wouldn't let go of her idea no matter what Samir said. "I shall make arrangements at once. We will have to inform the royal press officer—"

"Mother!" Samir snapped, his harsh tone finally

making her look at him. "I don't want a spouse," he repeated, more softly. "I really don't."

His mother sighed. "Darling," she said, laying a hand on his shoulder. "That's exactly what you need, trust me on that. I want you to be happy. You need to forget about the—the infatuation you have for Emyr's son. And for that, you'll need to make an effort to meet other people. An effort to fall in love with them. Forget about Warrehn'ngh'zaver. He isn't worth it. If you truly mattered to him..." She cocked her head to the side, eyeing him carefully. "If he *loved* you, he would never have given up on you just because your mother killed his parents and he doesn't trust you."

"Just because?" Samir muttered. "I can't believe you're so flippant about murdering his *parents*."

His mother shrugged. "Perhaps. But my point is, his feelings aren't strong enough." Something shifted about her expression. "If I killed Emyr's family, that wouldn't make him give me up. I know that for a fact."

Samir gave her a skeptical look. "Even if you're correct, that wouldn't prove that he loves you. That would only prove that he's sick and you're his illness. True love should be based on mutual trust and support." He swallowed around the thickness in his throat. "But yes, ultimately you're right that Warrehn doesn't love me. He made himself clear."

"I'm glad you understand it. So shall I proceed with the announcement?"

Samir winced. "Mother—"

"You asked me to leave Warrehn alone. I will abide by your request, but only if you abide by mine."

Samir frowned, searching his mother's face. She seemed serious.

"Fine," he said with a sigh.
His mother smiled, her eyes glinting with triumph.
Samir was already regretting it.

Chapter 21

Warrehn was in a dark mood when he left his office in the afternoon. He'd been in his office since last night, figuring he might as well do something productive if he couldn't sleep. Except the day had been largely unproductive. Everything pissed him off, and he'd ended up scaring away his assistants.

He craved some peace and quiet in his head, but he didn't think it was possible, not when he was this worked up and angry. He wasn't even sure who he was angrier with: his father, Dalatteya, Samir, or himself.

She's worried I have gotten attached to you.

The words played on a loop in his head, making it hard to focus on anything else. It was disturbing how badly he wanted to believe them, discarding all common sense, and it was doubly disturbing considering that the drug was gone from his system. He had checked with the doctor, twice. He had no one to blame for these obsessive thoughts but himself.

Warrehn came to an abrupt halt, frowning as he entered the palace's hall. It was full of flowers and gifts, of all kinds and sizes.

"What is this?" Warrehn said, surveying the room with a frown.

"The gifts are for Prince Samir, Your Majesty," a robot-maid said cheerfully. "Aww, are they not lovely?"

Warrehn stared at her, wondering who had thought that it was a good idea to give a robot a personality like this, before walking to the closest flower monstrosity and picking up the note.

I have long admired you, and my regard for you knows no bounds. I hope you accept my courtship.
-Zhangir'ngh'sekur

His forehead wrinkling, Warrehn plucked another note, and then another. They were much the same: some flowery nonsense and offers of courtship.

"The fuck," Warrehn said, crushing the note in his hand. He looked at the sea of flowers and bit the inside of his cheek hard, trying to suppress the violent urge to throw them all out and order the servants to do the same if they received more.

But he had no right. The drug debacle was over. Samir was nothing to him now. He was *worse* than nothing. He was his enemy's son. Completely off-limits. The ugly possessiveness in his chest was just the last aftereffect of the drug. It was. It had to be.

"Please put the note back," said a familiar female voice. "We wouldn't want my son not to receive it before he chooses a spouse."

Warrehn turned around and forced a blank look onto his face. He wouldn't give that woman the satisfaction of getting under his skin. "Pardon?"

Dalatteya smiled. "Oh, have you not heard yet? We formally announced this morning that the House of Lavette is accepting proposals of marriage for Samir."

Warrehn stared at her, struggling to keep his expression neutral.

Dalatteya's smile widened. "Perhaps I should have informed you personally. After all, as the head of the Fifth Royal House, you will be the one giving Samir away on his wedding day."

Warrehn had never been so tempted to hit a woman.

"Wedding day," he repeated.

Dalatteya nodded genially. "Obviously, since Samir won't have a childhood bond with his intended, the wedding rites will be more simplified than the traditional ones. I still fully plan to make it a grand affair." She looked Warrehn in the eyes. "My son deserves only the very best."

Warrehn gave her a flat look. "I don't know what this new scheme of yours is supposed to accomplish, but I have no intention of playing along."

"It might be hard to believe for such a self-centered man, but not everything is about you, Your Majesty," Dalatteya said coldly, the pretense of geniality gone. "There is no 'scheme.' My son is getting married soon. That has nothing to do with you." Her gaze turned positively icy. "Stay away from my son and don't ruin his future. Your behavior yesterday created enough rumors as it is—it would have been harmful if I weren't there to handle the issue. Keep your distance from Samir or *else*."

Warrehn clasped his balled fists behind his back. "I advise you not to threaten me, ma'am. You are forgetting yourself. I'm your king and you depend on my generosity. Samir is my subject and a member of the royal family. You cannot tell me to stay away from him. If I choose to stay away from him, it'll be my decision, not yours."

Dalatteya eyed him carefully, cocking her head to the side. She really looked a lot like Samir, just softer in her appearance, but that softness was very deceptive. Samir's eyes were kinder, lovelier. Dalatteya's were sharp as razors.

"You do want him," she said thoughtfully. "It's a pity I didn't believe Samir when he suggested seducing you to make you abdicate. The plan seemed outlandish when Samir suggested it, but now I see that I should have given him more time before exposing him yesterday."

Warrehn's stomach clenched, and it was a struggle to keep his face impassive. "I don't believe a word you say," he said flatly. "Get out of my sight."

Smiling, Dalatteya turned away and glided out of the room.

When she was gone, Warrehn slammed his fist against the nearest vase.

It broke, shattering into hundreds of pieces.

***

He didn't want to believe Dalatteya.

He told himself that she was lying, just trying to rile him up after he pointed out that she couldn't keep him away from Samir if he wanted otherwise.

But no matter what he told himself, that woman's words kept poisoning his thoughts, making him doubt himself, and doubt his perceptions. Doubt Samir's sincerity.

Although he had told Samir that he couldn't trust him, the aggravating truth was, Warrehn *did*. He knew he shouldn't trust him, but he had still been convinced that Samir wasn't like Dalatteya. But what if he was just seeing what he wanted to see? It was hard to believe that the person who felt so good to hold in his arms, with his lovely, warm smiles couldn't be what he seemed, that he could be plotting against him behind his back—but Emyr probably had thought the same about Dalatteya.

Had he been just deluding himself thinking that he was smarter than his father? Maybe he was repeating his father's mistakes. The thought was gut-wrenching.

To make things worse, doubting Samir's sincerity didn't stop him from being extremely aggravated by the gifts Samir kept receiving.

Warrehn had never agreed with the notion that power necessarily corrupted. At least he'd never thought he'd be one of those men who used their power to control other people's lives. But now he had to actively quash the urge to order the servants to throw out every single one of those gifts—and then lock Samir up in his room, and throw out the key.

If I can't have him, no one can.

His own thoughts creeped him out, but he couldn't seem to stop thinking shit like that. He'd never experienced this particular mix of emotions: anger, confusion, betrayal, and toxic possessiveness that didn't let him think clearly.

Even if Samir was a lying, traitorous thing, he was *Warrehn's*, no one else's. It was the single truth his mind didn't find some way to tangle, regardless of the feelings of anger and betrayal.

Warrehn heaved a sigh and sagged back in his seat, pinching the bridge of his nose.

Aftereffect of the drug or not, this toxic possessiveness was unacceptable. He was the king. He shouldn't have been wasting his time keeping tabs on what Samir was doing or how many gifts he was receiving instead of handling the hundred other, infinitely more important matters that required his attention.

Samir was the son of the woman who had murdered his family, and he had possibly been lying to him and conspiring to remove him from the throne. That should have been the end of it. Should have been.

It had been twenty hours since he'd last seen him.

Warrehn was annoyed with himself for knowing that. It was a bad habit he needed to break. There wasn't any alien drug in his system anymore. He had no excuse for this obsessive behavior. He should stop thinking about Samir all the time.

Unfortunately, it was easier said than done. The mere idea that Samir was considering marrying someone, that someone else would touch him, kiss him, hold him, have him under them—it was—

Warrehn swore under his breath and rolled his chair away from the desk, disgusted with himself.

"Damn you," he muttered, getting to his feet and marching out of the room.

He had intended to go outside. Clear his head with some fresh air.

But then he was informed by the palace AI that Samir was entertaining callers, and no amount of rational reasoning could have stopped Warrehn from heading there.

"His Majesty the King," the AI announced as Warrehn strode into the drawing room.

There were eight male and three female guests.

They all bowed to Warrehn—no, not all of them. The striking woman by Samir's side remained standing upright, proud and poised.

Recognizing her, Warrehn gave a clipped nod. He knew he should have bowed—that was the etiquette. She was the Queen of the First Grand Clan, and she took precedence over all the other monarchs of the planet.

Warrehn barely looked at her face.

His gaze was on her hand touching Samir's bicep, her manicured fingers wrapped around it possessively. Or at least it seemed possessive to Warrehn's eyes, but he was willing to admit that his judgment might be a little compromised. Or more than a little.

It took him an incredible effort not to stalk over to them and yank Samir away from Queen Kadira's grip. Since when was Queen Kadira looking for a spouse anyway? She'd always said that she was perfectly content to be alone after her husband had died in an accident. She was also more than twenty years older than Samir, closer in age to his mother—though the age difference didn't show yet. She was still beautiful.

Taking a deep breath, he shifted his gaze to Samir's face. Blue eyes met his, wide-eyed and a little wary, but so very soft. So very lovely. It pissed Warrehn off, the way one look completely disarmed him and made him want to stare into Samir's eyes like a besotted fool.

Was Dalatteya lying? He *needed* to know.

"Social hour is over," he said, glancing at the guests in the room.

His eyes widening, Samir shot him a scandalized look. "Um, I'm sure His Majesty didn't mean it that way—"

"I meant exactly what I said," Warrehn said. "I need to talk to you. Tell your guests to leave."

He walked to the window and stared out of it, waiting for everyone to vacate the room. He could see in his peripheral vision that the guests were exchanging stunned looks at his rudeness.

He didn't care. They had no idea how much restraint he was showing by not yanking Samir away from Queen Kadira and not kicking them all out in a much ruder fashion.

When the last guest finally vacated the room, Samir made an exasperated sound. "Are you crazy? That was beyond rude!"

Warrehn turned and stalked over.

He didn't know what expression was on his face, but Samir's expression became wary.

He stopped in front of Samir, their faces just a palm's width apart, and watched Samir swallow.

"Queen Kadira, huh?" Warrehn said. "It's disgusting. She's your mother's age."

Flushing, Samir glared at him. "She isn't. She's just forty-six. And that's none of your business."

It was annoying how pretty he was when he was angry. Warrehn wanted to wrap his hands around that pale, lovely neck and *strangle* him, for turning him into an obsessive, possessive fool who couldn't stop wanting him even if he'd been betrayed.

"My point stands," Warrehn said. "She could have been your mother. But then again, you probably like it."

Samir narrowed his eyes. "What is that supposed to mean?"

"Ever heard of the Oedipus complex? You're a grown man who still does everything your mommy says. It makes me wonder sometimes about your relationship with your mother."

Samir punched him. Warrehn caught his wrist and pushed it behind Samir's back, pulling them flush against each other. Fuck, he wanted to shove him down to his knees and ram his cock into Samir's throat, Dalatteya and Samir's possible treachery be damned. Samir was his. *His,* not Dalatteya's, not Queen Kadira's, or anyone else's. His.

"Let go!" Samir was all but spitting. "How dare you, to insinuate that—that—"

"Get on your knees."

Samir shot him a half-incredulous, half-furious look. "You're out of your mind if you think I'll suck your cock after you just insinuated that I want to fuck my mother. Even if I marry Queen Kadira, that's none of your damn business! I will marry whoever I want."

"Get on your knees," Warrehn repeated. "You will get on your knees and suck your king's cock."

Samir flushed again, his lips parting. His gaze flicked down to Warrehn's crotch.

"You can't make me," Samir said, his pink tongue darting out to lick his full lips, as if he had no idea what he was doing to him.

Or maybe he knew exactly what he was doing to him. Maybe his innocent looks were just a facade. Maybe he was as treacherous as Dalatteya, and Warrehn had been a fool, a fool like his father. The thought made him angry enough to bit off, "I can't? I'm your king. Isn't it your duty to service your king?"

Samir's pupils dilated, his breath quickening. "I…" He swallowed. "The door isn't even locked. One of the guests might return."

A nasty wave of possessiveness made him grind out, "Good. Kneel."

His throat moving, Samir stared at Warrehn, before slowly dropping to his knees. He unzipped Warrehn's fly with trembling fingers, the sound obscenely loud in the quiet room.

Warrehn's cock sprang out of his fly, red and leaking. Samir stared at it for a moment with glazed eyes before leaning in and licking the head. It felt like heaven, but Warrehn didn't want false-gentleness. He wanted to fuck that mouth just like Samir had fucked him up.

He grabbed Samir's head with both hands and slammed his cock into his mouth.

Samir moaned, choking on his length, and it drove Warrehn absolutely crazy. He pulled out and thrust back in, groaning at the slick heat around him, and angry for wanting this so much. But it was bliss, to fuck that sweet, lying mouth out here, in the open, where anyone could come across them and see who fucking *owned* Samir.

When he looked down, he saw that Samir had his fly open and was stroking his own cock, fast and desperate while Warrehn fucked his mouth. Possible treachery or not, at least he was getting off on this. Slut. Whore. Traitor.

Their eyes met, and Warrehn stared into those wide, lovely eyes, all the nasty thoughts forgotten. He wanted to drop to his knees and worship him, take him into his arms and tell him how much he—

How much he loved him.

He came, spilling deep into Samir's throat.

His hands shaking, Warrehn yanked his zipper up and strode out of the room, freaked out of his mind.

Chapter 22

"And then your spawn had the nerve to say that I depend on his generosity!" Dalatteya seethed, pacing the room. "If it weren't for Samir, if my son didn't get stupidly attached to that odious man, I would destroy him, but now my hands are tied and I'm forced to make nice with your spawn!" She stopped pacing and put her hands on her hips. "Are you even listening to me?"

Emyr hummed, his eyes still on his book. "Of course, pet. I always listen to you. You're simply not saying anything of note. I expected this to happen."

She narrowed her eyes, a sinking feeling appearing in her stomach. "You expected this to happen?" she said slowly.

Emyr lifted his gaze, seemingly bored. But Dalatteya knew him. She could see the subtle expression of triumph glinting in those blue eyes.

He shrugged.

She wasn't fooled. "What did you do?" she said, her heart beating faster.

Emyr leaned back in his chair and regarded her for a moment. "Uriel didn't make a mistake," he said, watching her like a scientist would watch a lab rat for a reaction. "You did order him to use the drug Uriel used on our sons."

Dalatteya shook her head. "That's impossible. I assure you I perfectly remember my conversations with Uriel, and he admitted that he'd made a mis—" She cut herself off, staring at Emyr. "You messed with my memories."

Emyr didn't even bother to confirm or deny it, just looked at her steadily.

Dalatteya's stomach clenched. So her conversations about the drug with Uriel… Had they even happened? She had been so sure Uriel apologized for the mistake. Had she even talked to him?

"Why?" she said.

"To protect my line," Emyr said. "I knew you would have my son killed, sooner or later, no matter how vigilant he was. The only solution was to make Samir want him alive—you wouldn't want to upset your precious son. The drug would have tied them together and bought Warrehn some time at the very least, and I calculated the likelihood of them getting attached to each other to be quite high, considering that they're both lonely and desperate for affection, and your son is undoubtedly as weak and soft as his father was."

A small smile curled Emyr's lips. "Stop looking at me that way, my dear. You should allow a prisoner some small amusements. Ruining your plans to end my line was just a bit of harmless fun."

"You…" Dalatteya shook her head, angry with herself for not expecting something like this. Even imprisoned and mostly powerless, Emyr was still one of the most dangerous men she'd ever met. It had been foolish of her to think that she could completely control him. "You messed with my mind. How do I know you aren't brainwashing me?"

She felt a surge of his bitterness through their bond. Glancing at his wrists, Emyr said flatly, "You ensured that my telepathy is so limited that it would be impossible even if I wanted to. Replacing some memories and putting protective mind traps is one thing; brainwashing is another. If I could brainwash you, I would have simply made you like my son or made you leave him alone. I would have made you release me. But alas. I had to work with the limited power I have."

He sighed. "Stop looking at me like I'm the monster here. It gets quite tiring, my love. You hardly have the moral high ground, when all I did was protect my son from getting murdered by you."

Dalatteya laughed. "Please. You don't care about your son, Emyr. All you care about is for *your* line to continue and you hate the idea of Aslehn's son taking your throne."

A muscle worked in Emyr's jaw. "Don't speak that man's name," he said evenly.

She scoffed and turned away, knowing that it would only infuriate Emyr.

After a few moments, she heard him set his book aside and get to his feet.

Then she felt him behind her, his tall, powerful body pressing against her back as his strong arms wrapped around her waist like a vise. She loathed how right it felt. How perfect.

Emyr brushed his lips against her neck. "I'm not like you," he said. "I never understood why you cared so much for that man's brat. I certainly didn't care for the children I had with my wife. I didn't contribute to their creation beyond jerking off into a cup, so I don't know why I should love them."

Dalatteya had known that. She had known that Emyr had never even slept with the queen-consort, which was the reason the woman hated Dalatteya so much. Truth be told, Dalatteya had almost pitied her. She couldn't imagine being bonded to a man who wouldn't even look at her, much less kiss her or touch her—being bonded to *Emyr* who didn't want her. Dalatteya would have pitied her if the woman hadn't tried to poison her multiple times and hadn't nearly killed Samir by mistake. The queen's behavior was doubly irrational, considering that she had no claim to Emyr beyond a document that said he was hers. He'd never been hers. Emyr had married her because he had to. Dalatteya knew she had been the only woman in his bed since he was eighteen.

Emyr's hand cradled her stomach possessively. He kissed her neck again and said hoarsely, "I would love my children if they were yours and mine."

She shivered. It wasn't the first time Emyr had expressed the thought over the decades, but she had always refused to stop taking her contraceptives. When her husband had been alive, the father of her child would have been immediately obvious, since she rarely shared Aslehn's bed. She had refused to make Aslehn suffer the additional offense of seeing her pregnant with the king's child.

But a part of her had always wondered what it would have been like, to bear Emyr's child—to bear any child. Samir was the product of artificial gestation in a genetic center, and while she loved him more than anything, she still would have liked to have carried him under her heart. But she had been deprived of that, because she had known Emyr would never have allowed her to get pregnant with another man's child—he resented Samir's existence as it was.

"My doctor has said I'm not fertile anymore, so you can stop entertaining those thoughts," Dalatteya said coldly, as if the news hadn't been a little disheartening to her.

"Has he?" Emyr murmured, trailing his hot mouth over her neck, her ear, his large hands sliding up to knead her breasts. "So you've stopped getting your shots?"

"They aren't needed anymore," she said, gasping as he pinched her nipples.

"They were never needed," he said, biting her earlobe and cupping her between her legs.

She moaned and didn't resist as he bent her over the desk and hiked her skirts up.

Chapter 23

Emyr'ngh'zaver
(18709-18750)
A caring king, a loving husband and father
May you rest in tranquility

His father's grave was in the center of the royal graveyard, among the other deceased monarchs of their clan. Contrary to the custom, the queen-consort's grave wasn't beside Emyr's. Warrehn vaguely remembered wondering about it when he had been ten, but back then, he had been too consumed by grief to make inquiries about who had given the order to bury the late queen in a different part of the graveyard.

He had a feeling he knew who. It would be just like Dalatteya to keep them apart even in death.

Warrehn sat down on the bench in front of the grave and stared at his father's proud profile blankly. He still remembered that day so clearly. The "tragic news." The "my condolences, Your Highness." Dalatteya's pale face with wide, unfocused eyes, her lips twisted in a strange expression that seemed like something between a smile and a sob. Her hand tightly gripping Samir's small hand.

His childhood had ended that day.

"I wonder what your last thoughts were," Warrehn said quietly. Unlike the queen-consort, Emyr hadn't died instantly. He'd been in a coma for a short while, with only Dalatteya beside him as he died in a hospital bed. "Did you even realize that she betrayed you? The woman you loved?"

The woman whose son Warrehn was in love with.

The thought was as maddening as it had been the first time it had occurred to him.

He couldn't love Samir.

But he did.

He couldn't trust Samir.

But he *did*. Regardless of his doubts, deep down, his besotted self refused to believe Samir was as treacherous as his mother. He might be freaking out because of Samir, but paradoxically, he wanted to hold him in his arms to feel better. His mind was always calm and at peace when he had Samir curled up in his arms.

He wondered if Emyr had felt the same about Dalatteya.

"Damn you, Father," Warrehn said with a hoarse chuckle. "I swore I wouldn't repeat your mistakes, but here I am."

He sat up straighter as he suddenly recalled the fleeting thought that had crossed his mind: Dalatteya had been at Emyr's bedside as he died.

They had been alone.

Warrehn's heart started beating faster.

Fuck, why hadn't he thought of it before? Emyr had been in a coma, allegedly dying, but what's to say it wasn't another lie and Dalatteya hadn't killed him while they were alone? He would have to look up the hospital's security feeds.

Hospitals never deleted security footage, archiving the videos in case they were needed in medical malpractice lawsuits—they could only be deleted by a special decree of the Council.

Which meant he might finally find proof of Dalatteya's crimes.

***

Getting access to the security footage from twenty years ago wasn't easy even for a king. Warrehn had to personally go to the hospital Emyr had died in, to intimidate them into granting him access.

Finally, after two frustrating hours of security checks, he had been allowed into the archives.

"You will be able to view only the footage that concerns your immediate family, Your Majesty," the technician reminded him timidly. "The videos are protected, and you will not be able to delete any of them without a special decree of the Council. You can copy some files—the system will automatically detect if you're authorized to do so."

Warrehn gave a curt nod. "I'm aware," he said. "You may go."

Once he was alone in the archives, Warrehn walked to the holoterminal and entered the date of his father's death.

Since there was a filter preventing him from viewing videos of other people, it didn't take him long to find the security footage from Emyr's hospital room.

His father had been cremated, as was custom. Warrehn hadn't seen his body at all—the doctors had advised against it, saying that the sight wasn't suitable for a ten-year-old child.

Now he understood what they had meant.

Warrehn bit the inside of his cheek, looking at the body in the hospital bed. He could barely see his father under the bloody bandages. His right arm was missing entirely. His face had fared better than the rest of him, but even his face had nasty burns and cuts. The doctors left the room one by one, shaking their heads and speaking in low voices, saying that there was no chance of recovery and the king's death was a matter of time now.

It nearly made him turn off the video. It was clear that Dalatteya was unlikely to have done anything to Emyr in the hospital: the man lying on that bed didn't need any additional help to die.

But as Warrehn reached to turn it off, Dalatteya entered the hospital room.

"My lady, you shouldn't be here," the doctor who had stayed in the room said.

She didn't even glance at him, her eyes on the man in the hospital bed. "Is he...?" she whispered.

The doctor sighed. "I'm sorry, my lady. We did everything we could. But His Majesty's injuries were too severe when he was brought here. There wasn't a single organ that wasn't severely damaged, half of his organs had already failed. It's frankly amazing he's still alive. It's just a matter of time now. I'm sorry."

"Leave me alone with him."

The doctor opened his mouth and closed it before nodding and leaving.

Dalatteya walked to the bed, her pale face devoid of any expression as her eyes roamed over the king's mutilated body. She wrapped her arms around herself, and Warrehn noticed that her hands were shaking.

Maybe she was nervous that someone would guess that she was the one behind the terrorist attack.

She whispered something, barely audibly. Warrehn frowned and, raising the volume, listened again.

"Look at you," she whispered. "Look how pathetic you look. Emyr'ngh'zaver. How the mighty have fallen. You're nothing but bones and blood. You lost. You—you— You never thought I had it in me, did you? But I won. I'm free. I'm—I'm—"

The beeping of the heart monitor became erratic— and then it stopped, flatlining.

Immediately, the doctors rushed in, but came to a halt.

"What's happening?" Dalatteya demanded, her eyes wide. "Why aren't you doing anything?"

The doctor closest to her said, "The king is dead, my lady."

Dalatteya looked at him blankly, as if she couldn't grasp the meaning of his words, before her head whipped back to the body and then to the other monitors.

"But—this one is still active!" she said, pointing at the monitor that still showed some activity. "He can't be—he can't be—"

"It's a psi-monitor, my lady," the doctor explained. "It shows his brain activity. The mind of a Calluvian dies last. Typically, the more powerful a telepath, the longer his mind will hang on even if his body is dead. The king was a powerful telepath. His brain activity likely won't cease for some time yet." The doctor bowed his head. "I'm sorry for your loss, my lady."

Dalatteya just stared at Emyr's body, her face devoid of any emotion. She remained still as a statue as the doctors left the room.

Then, a horrible noise left her throat, something between a sob and a choke.

Warrehn stared at her, puzzled. Why was she still not dropping the act? There was no one there.

He watched in confusion as Dalatteya suddenly lifted her head, her eyes flashing, as if an idea occurred to her. She pulled out her communicator, and said, "Uriel, I need you to get something for me, now. I'll message you what I want." She typed something, her expression resolute. Then she put the communicator back in her purse and retrieved a pair of manicure scissors out of it.

"What are you doing?" Warrehn murmured as he watched her cut a few strands of his father's hair and hide it in her bodice.

Then she walked to the psi-activity monitor and stared at it with an empty, thousand-yard stare. Her throat kept bobbing, as if she was swallowing something—or struggling to breathe. Otherwise, her expression remained creepily blank.

At long last, a man in a doctor's coat entered the room. Warrehn frowned, recognizing Dalatteya's current head of security, Uriel. Why was he disguised as a doctor? Why had she summoned him?

"My lady?" Uriel said, glancing around nervously. "I've managed to acquire what you requested, but are you sure? If we're caught, it'll be a life sentence—"

"Get to work," Dalatteya said tonelessly, still looking at the psi-monitor. "We don't have much time."

Uriel looked very much unhappy with her order, but he didn't argue and pulled out some device from the briefcase he had brought.

His frown deepening, Warrehn eyed the unfamiliar device.

Something tugged at his memory—perhaps he had seen it somewhere—but it didn't click until Uriel placed the device on Emyr's telepathic point.

Warrehn swore elaborately, stunned and furious in equal measure. So apparently it hadn't been enough for Dalatteya to kill his parents, she had also had to steal Emyr's mind as well.

That device—the mind vortex—was outlawed on Calluvia for a reason. It had been invented thousands of years ago, when a dying king of the Ninth Grand Clan had decided to cheat death and transplant his mind into that of a young, cloned body. A legal nightmare followed: was the clone entitled to rule or should the king's heir inherit? The legal dispute had turned into a long, messy, bloody civil war that nearly wiped out the entire clan. Afterward, the Council of Grand Clans had outlawed the mind vortex: using it on common people was twenty years in prison, and using it on members of nobility and royalty was a life sentence for everyone involved—and clones couldn't rule or inherit. Rich commoners still used the device: what was twenty years in prison compared to a second life? But royals? There was no point, so it hadn't happened in thousands of years.

Until apparently Dalatteya had done it twenty years ago. *Why?*

Warrehn struggled to think of a reason.

"My lady," Uriel tried again. "Please rethink this—"

"No," Dalatteya said, her eyes glinting. "Do as I say. I need him—need his mind. It'll be useful, you'll see. His knowledge is invaluable."

On the screen, Emyr's psi-activity ceased.

Dalatteya made a punched-out noise, her eyes glazing over as she staggered on her feet, swaying a little.

Warrehn frowned, wondering if she had shared some kind of mental bond with Emyr.

"Have you—have you managed to finish the transfer?" she croaked out.

"Yes, my lady."

Dalatteya closed her eyes and nodded. "Let's go," she said tonelessly. "We need to leave before the palace officials come."

Uriel glanced straight into the camera, swallowing. "But what about the security footage, milady? I will not be able to wipe it."

Dalatteya's shoulders tensed before relaxing again. "The videos are automatically privacy-locked. Only his immediate family can access the files. And that would be Emyr's sons, and they are children. It shouldn't be an issue."

"And what if the eldest boy starts asking questions and wishes to see his father's last moments?"

Dalatteya's lips thinned. "If it happens, we'll handle it."

Warrehn shook his head. So many things made sense now. All these years, he had wondered why Dalatteya had decided to kill him when he had started asking questions about the circumstances around his father's death. Why had she been scared of a child? But this finally made it make sense. Warrehn had been the only one besides a three-year-old Eri who could access this video, which was undeniable proof of Dalatteya's guilt—even if it was of a different crime than the one Warrehn had expected.

It didn't matter. This footage would be enough to get her locked up for all the things she had done.

Warrehn inserted a holochip into the terminal, and pressed Copy.

Chapter 24

Warrehn had considered doing it publicly at first. There was a certain degree of satisfaction in having the bitch arrested in a public setting, in front of hundreds of eyewitnesses, and have her flawless public image ruined.

But he was loath to air their dirty laundry in front of the court. Loath to have to show everyone his father's last moments, the way he had been desecrated even after his death. It didn't matter that the clone had likely been dead for decades now; the fact that Dalatteya had temporarily given Emyr's mind a new body to torture information out of him was… It turned Warrehn's stomach. His father had hardly been perfect, but even he didn't deserve that fate. No one did.

So he sent messages to all the relevant people to come to his office.

Eridan was the first to arrive. "What's happening, War?" he said, brushing his telepathic presence against his in a mental hug. "Your message was confusing."

Warrehn had been vague on purpose when he'd messaged Eridan. He didn't want anything to leak prematurely—he didn't trust people at the High Hronthar—but his brother deserved to be present as the woman who had murdered their parents and who was responsible for the attack on them was finally arrested for her crimes.

"I found proof," he said.

Eridan's eyes widened. "Really?"

Warrehn nodded, but before either of them could say anything, the door opened and Fariz announced the Lord Chancellor's arrival. Ksar walked in, accompanied by two law enforcement officials.

"Thanks for coming," Warrehn said. He wouldn't have taken offense if Ksar had declined handling this case: he knew Ksar was leaving for a long-awaited vacation with his husband later that day. Being involved in such a messy case was probably the last thing he needed before his departure. Strictly speaking, Ksar was a little overqualified for this—any high-ranking official of the Ministry would have sufficed—but Warrehn wanted to be sure that the Ministry official in charge of the case wasn't in Dalatteya's pocket. He didn't want to leave anything to chance. Ksar was the Lord Chancellor of the planet and a future king of the Second Grand Clan; there wasn't a man more powerful on the planet outside of Idhron. He certainly wasn't in anyone's pocket, and he had proven to be an ally in the past.

"I have only an hour at most," Ksar said, nodding in answer to Eridan's greeting before his silver eyes focused on Warrehn. "Are you certain you want to do it? It will be messy and unpleasant for everyone involved once the news spreads."

Warrehn gave a curt nod. Regardless of the upcoming scandal, he couldn't let his parents' murderer continue to walk free.

The door open and Dalatteya entered—followed by Samir.

His heart beating faster, Warrehn snapped his gaze away, knowing that if he met Samir's eyes, he wouldn't be able to focus on anything else and think rationally. He was distracted already, his body acutely aware of Samir's every movement.

Don't be a fool. He's Dalatteya's son. The son of the woman you're getting arrested. Even if he doesn't hate you now, he will, in a very short time.

"What is the meaning of this?" Dalatteya said coldly. "I'm not a servant to be summoned without any explanation." A flicker of confusion and wariness appeared in her eyes once she noticed the presence of the law enforcement officials and Ksar. "Your Royal Highness," she said with a graceful bow. "I wasn't aware you called on us."

"It's not a social visit," Warrehn said. "Sit. All of you."

When everyone sat down, Warrehn said, looking at Dalatteya, "The Lord Chancellor is here in the capacity of a Ministry official to record and file the charges against you, as is procedure. I could have gone to the Council with this, but I know you have a lot of support there and I don't trust them to carry out justice."

Not a single muscle moved on Dalatteya's face, but her telepathic presence coiled tightly, emanating anxiety. "I have no idea what you mean."

In his peripheral vision, Samir shifted. Quashing the urge to look at him, Warrehn looked at Ksar. "Are you recording?"

Ksar gave a nod, touching the chip on his wrist.

Warrehn looked back at Dalatteya, feeling a surge of dark satisfaction as something like panic appeared in her eyes.

In the meantime, Ksar said, "Dalatteya'il'zaver, you are charged with multiple murders, treason, fraud, five occasions of attempted murder, and the use of mind vortex on the deceased king, Emyr'ngh'zaver."

Dalatteya paled. There were several gasps in the room, and Warrehn's gaze flicked to Dalatteya's right. Samir was staring at his mother, his lovely eyes wide and confused.

See, he's innocent, his besotted self immediately argued.

Grimacing inwardly, Warrehn wrenched his gaze away. Now wasn't the time for acting like a lovesick fool. Whether Samir knew of the mind vortex or not was largely irrelevant and didn't prove his innocence. He'd been a child back then; of course he hadn't been involved. It meant nothing and didn't mean he hadn't been involved in Dalatteya's other plans.

"This is the most ridiculous thing I've ever heard!" Dalatteya said, springing to her feet. "I will not listen to this nonsense!"

"Sit down, ma'am," Ksar said, his voice like ice. When she reluctantly sat down, he said, "The accusations are not baseless. The Ministry has been presented with conclusive proof of your use of a mind vortex." He touched his wrist and a holovid of the security footage Warrehn had retrieved appeared in the air.

Warrehn didn't look at it. He watched the others' reactions. Eridan looked sickened when he saw the mind vortex, Ksar's face was impassive, and Samir... Samir turned to look at his mother with an expression of dawning horror on his face.

"Mother..." he whispered hoarsely, shaking his head. "How could you have been so stupid? So reckless? That's a life sentence!"

Dalatteya pursed her lips tightly and said nothing, her gaze empty. Defeated. Her eyes remained on the image of Emyr's dead, mutilated body.

Warrehn got to his feet and stepped closer to her. "What did you do to it?"

"It?" she repeated blankly.

"The clone. Did you even bury it after you tortured the information you wanted out of it?"

She looked back at Emyr's body and said nothing.

Getting to his feet as well, Ksar broke the silence. "It's over, ma'am. The other charges against you will be investigated, but the use of the mind vortex alone is grounds for immediate arrest. Your head of security will be arrested too, once he's found." He glanced at the law enforcement officials. "Arrest her."

Dalatteya didn't resist, still looking at Emyr's dead body.

"No," Samir choked out as his mother was put in handcuffs. "No!" He turned and grabbed Warrehn's hands. "Please," he said hoarsely, looking at him with glistening eyes. "Warrehn." He fell to his knees and whispered, "I'm begging you."

"Get up, Samir," Dalatteya said sharply. "You're above begging—especially begging that man."

Samir ignored her, looking at Warrehn pleadingly, still on his knees. "Please. She's my mother."

Warrehn dragged his gaze away and glowered at the gawking officials, shielding Samir from their view with his body.

"Everyone out," he ordered, before pushing a thought at Ksar, *Make sure they don't talk and the news doesn't spread yet.*

Ksar gave a curt nod and walked out of the room, his men following with Dalatteya. Eridan lingered, looking at them for a moment, before leaving too.

And then they were alone. He and the man he loved—and whose mother he'd just condemned to a life sentence.

Chapter 25

Samir had never felt so desperate. Desperate and scared. His mother was arrested. And the use of a mind vortex was a life sentence, no appeal possible. She was going to spend the rest of her life on one of the prison planets, those disease-ridden, horrible places that used the prisoners as free labor in the mines. He couldn't imagine his delicate, graceful mother in a place like that, among the worst sort of criminals. With her looks, it would be a living hell. She would be gang-raped on a daily basis.

"Get up," Warrehn said, without looking at him.

Samir searched his hard face for a hint of kindness and mercy. He couldn't find it.

"Don't do it, War. Please."

Warrehn finally looked at him, a muscle jumping in his cheek. "Don't," he said roughly. "She isn't worth your tears. She's a heartless killer without any principles."

"She's my mother," Samir whispered, squeezing Warrehn's hands with his own. "She's all I had growing up."

"And she's the reason my mother is dead," Warrehn said flatly, without looking at him. "She's the reason my father was killed and then tortured even after his death. She's the reason my brother grew up in a miserable place like the High Hronthar, all alone." *She's the reason I don't have a family.*

Samir's heart clenched as he caught the stray thought Warrehn involuntarily projected. "I know she's done bad things," he breathed, leaning his forehead against Warrehn's hard thigh and closing his burning eyes. "I know that, and I'm sorry. I'm really, really sorry. But I can't stop loving her. For me, she was the best mother in the world. She's always been there for me."

He took a death breath, trying to regain his composure, but he'd never felt so shaky and uncertain. He yearned to feel Warrehn's hand in his hair, his arms around him, but Warrehn was so rigid against him. At least he wasn't pushing him away. "You asked me what happened to my bondmate. I'll tell you what happened." Samir bit his bottom lip hard. "Malik's childhood bond to me was somewhat faulty. It didn't repress his sexual urges. When we turned thirteen, he started being—pushy. I said no, I said I was uncomfortable, but he only became more insistent with the years. When we were fifteen, we went on a hike in the mountains. And he started—he started—you know."

Warrehn stiffened further. Samir exhaled shakily. "I said no, but he wouldn't listen. I shoved him off me." He swallowed the lump in his throat. "He staggered back— and fell off the edge. It was an accident, I swear! I didn't mean to kill him. But I did. I killed him."

"Samir," Warrehn said, laying a hand on his head, his voice rough. "He brought it on himself. It was self-defense. It was an accident."

"Mother said the same thing," Samir said, unable to look at him.

Fuck, what he wouldn't give to be wrapped up in Warrehn's arms and squeezed tightly, to feel that wonderful *safe-secure-protected* feeling.

"I was inconsolable after Malik's death. He was my best friend. We grew up together. Feeling our bond physically snap as he fell down the mountain was—" Samir had to swallow again. "I lost it. I cried for days. I didn't want to leave my bed or eat or drink. Mother literally spoon-fed me, sang me lullabies and held me as if I were a baby. If it weren't for her, I would have never recovered. And if it weren't for her, I would have been exposed as a murderer, just like my mother."

"You aren't a murderer," Warrehn said, his tone hard. "It was self-defense. Dalatteya's actions were done in cold blood. She killed not only her assaulter, but an innocent woman—and then tried to kill children."

"She did it for me, Warrehn," Samir said softly. "Everything my mother did was done for me. Even the king's death… I'm pretty sure she would have never killed him if she weren't scared for my life."

"What? It doesn't make sense."

"It does. Mother once told me that King Emyr was unhealthily possessive of her and hated that she had a child with another man, that he hated my existence and her love for me. I think after Emyr killed my father, she started fearing for my life, too."

"You're reading too much into it. Dalatteya hated him and wanted him dead. That's the end of it."

Samir lifted his head and met his blue eyes. "I'm pretty sure my mother loved him. It was a toxic, unhealthy love—she both hated him and loved him. He was the center of her world either way. And she gave him up for me."

Warrehn chuckled, shaking his head. "That's ridiculous. She hated him."

"I wish," Samir said, thinking of how empty and broken his mother had looked when she saw the king's dead body in the video. "Haven't you just seen the way she looked at Emyr's mutilated body? It wasn't the look of someone who hated him. I think his death was enough of a punishment for her."

A deep furrow appeared between Warrehn's brows, but he clearly remained unconvinced.

Samir sighed and got to his feet. Immediately, he felt so much colder. And so very alone.

Warrehn's hand twitched toward him, and Samir felt a desperate flicker of hope that he would be touched and held and *crushed* in those arms.

But Warrehn put his hands on the desk behind him and gripped the edge hard, his jaw setting. He eyed Samir for a moment. "Your mother told me that you were planning to seduce me to talk me into abdicating."

Samir's stomach plummeted. He winced and shook his head. "It was her idea. I told her it would never work. No one would give up the throne for some base lust. You'd have to have feelings for me. Like, deep feelings." He smiled crookedly. "Which is obviously ridiculous."

Something shifted in Warrehn's blue eyes. "But you still went along with the plan."

"No, I didn't," Samir said, pulling a face. "Well, I tried, very briefly, at the beginning, but you saw right through me." He frowned. "Is that why you were so angry yesterday?" He was relieved. Although the whole thing had been a turn-on, Warrehn had never treated him so cruelly before. Knowing that he'd been angry because he thought Samir had betrayed him was—it was a relief.

"You think I had no right to be angry when the man I'm in—" Warrehn cut himself off and averted his gaze.

Samir stared at him, his heart starting to beat faster. Did he…?

"Warrehn?" he said softly.

His expression pinched, Warrehn looked at him, then looked away again, his jaw working. "I wanted to hate you," he said at last, his voice tight and rough. "You're Dalatteya's son. That's all you should have been."

Samir took a step closer. "War?" he said, lifting his hand and touching Warrehn's stubbled cheek. His fingers were unsteady, he felt almost dizzy from the mad hope coursing through him. "Do you…?"

"I should hate you," Warrehn said, catching his fingers with his larger hand and kissing his knuckles one by one, his mouth hot and reverent.

A small noise slipped out of Samir's mouth. He gasped, pressing his trembling fingertips against Warrehn's lips.

"I shouldn't trust you," Warrehn said, his other arm wrapping around Samir's waist and crushing him to him. Samir whimpered, his mind going blissfully empty as the *safe-perfect-protected* feeling he'd craved so much was back.

"I shouldn't," Warrehn said, tucking Samir's head under his chin and hugging him hard. "But I do, damn you." He buried his face in Samir's hair. "I know it's irrational. I have no proof of your loyalties. But I hate seeing you upset. I hate seeing your tears. They make me feel guilty for arresting your mother, even though she deserves it a hundred times over. You have no idea how much it fucks with my head—how much you fucked me up and changed my priorities."

Samir couldn't breathe.

He felt like his heart was about to burst out of his chest.

He cradled Warrehn's face with his hands and kissed him hard, pouring everything into the kiss.

I'm sorry, Mother, he thought, his eyes stinging. *But I love him. I love him so much.* He was done being in denial. If he could still feel this way for a man who had sentenced his mother to a fate worse than death, it could only be love.

And if he couldn't save his mother, at least he could save this fragile, precious feeling between them.

Taking Warrehn's hand, Samir moved it to his telepathic point.

"Please," he said against Warrehn's mouth. "Do it. Merge us."

Warrehn went rigid against him, their breaths mixing. "You have no idea what you're asking for. Merging with me is dangerous. You have no experience. I'm a Class Six telepath, Samir."

Samir froze and pulled back a little, looking at him wide-eyed. He had suspected that Warrehn was strong, but he had thought he was a Four, maybe a Five at most. A Six was... he could do a lot of damage to Samir in a merge if he was careless.

He didn't believe Warrehn would be careless.

"I trust you," he said, holding Warrehn's gaze. "I want you to trust me, too."

Warrehn's expression softened. He *smiled* at him, the smile making him breathtakingly handsome. "I don't need a merge to trust you. That's the problem."

Samir felt a little choked up. He looped his arms around Warrehn's neck and smiled at him, feeling so besotted that for a moment he didn't know what to say. "I insist. I want us to get to know each other on the deepest level. I don't want you to feel bad about trusting me. I don't want there to be even a shadow of doubt."

Warrehn studied him awhile before nodding. "Let me know if you're uncomfortable, all right?"

Samir gave a small nod and closed his eyes when Warrehn's hand touched his telepathic point below his ear.

He didn't know what he had expected. He'd heard that telepathic merges were incredibly overwhelming. He'd heard that they were very invasive, even unsettling.

But it was none of those things.

It was like feeling the fresh breeze on your face after a long and tiresome day. It was like getting into your soft, comfortable bed after barely sleeping for a month. It was like coming home.

He shivered in delight as he felt Warrehn slip deeper and deeper into his mind. He could feel Warrehn's every emotion, and he knew Warrehn was feeling his, so he opened himself up, unashamed and hungry for more, hungry for this man in ways that went beyond physical need. When Warrehn finally reached his telepathic core, Samir heard himself moan—it felt so good, he couldn't even describe it. Warrehn stroked his core, faster and deeper, until he felt like he exploded into a million pieces, the pleasure so intense and unlike any he'd felt before, and it went on, and on, and on.

He didn't know how much time had passed when he regained his ability to think. The merge felt less intense now, but no less addictive: he could feel Warrehn so intimately it was like they were one person. He could feel how lonely Warrehn had been all his life, the hollowness inside him that yearned for something to call his. A family. Something that had been stolen from him.

It made Samir incredibly sad—and incredibly thrilled and honored when he realized that he was the one thing Warrehn regarded as his now. The only person who filled the hole inside Warrehn's chest and made him feel at peace.

What about Eridan? Samir asked softly through the merge.

He's Idhron's, Warrehn replied. *You're* mine.

There was such force in that sentiment, it made Samir shiver. *Yours,* he confirmed, even though it was unneeded: Warrehn could feel everything he felt and knew how much he liked the idea. It should have felt scary, to bare his soul and mind that way to another person. It wasn't. He liked being vulnerable, liked being vulnerable with *this* man, the absolute trust, the rush of fear and then acceptance, the *I see you.*

I'm sorry, Warrehn said. *About your mother. I understand now, but…*

I know, Samir said. He now understood, too, having felt Warrehn's grief like his own. Samir loved his mother, but Warrehn had loved his own mother, too, the beautiful, golden-haired woman with sad, unsmiling eyes. That woman might have tried to kill Dalatteya and felt nothing but malice toward her, but she had been a good mother. And she deserved justice. *I understand, War. It's fine.*

It wasn't fine, not really, but Warrehn knew what he meant and wrapped him in a tight mental embrace that mirrored the physical hug he was giving him. Samir sighed, clinging to him, both sad and happy. At least they had each other. They always would.

"Your Majesty? Your Majesty!"

Warrehn dropped his hand from Samir's telepathic point and the merge snapped.

Samir made a punched-out noise, feeling disoriented and so very alone in his head. Thankfully, the arms around him grounded him, and he exhaled, relaxing, and opened his eyes.

The first thing he saw were Warrehn's blue eyes.

There was concern in them, but there was a new softness and warmth too. "All right?" Warrehn said quietly, stroking his back.

Samir nodded, smiling. He was more than all right.

But then he frowned, noticing the dark sky outside the window behind Warrehn. How was it possible? It had been morning.

"We lost a lot of time in the merge," Warrehn explained, stroking his back absently. His brows were furrowed in bemusement. "It happens sometimes, though it never happened to me before."

"Your Majesty," the AI said again.

"What is it?" Warrehn said with an irritated sigh, his gaze still on Samir.

"There was a call from the Ministry. They said it was urgent."

Warrehn exchanged a look with Samir, and Samir shrugged, unsure what to think.

"Did they leave a message?"

"Yes, Your Majesty."

"Play it," Warrehn said, brushing his lips against Samir's temple.

"One moment, Your Majesty."

A hologram appeared in the air. It was a man wearing the Ministry's uniform.

"Your Majesty, Dalatteya'il'zaver escaped."

Chapter 26

Warrehn wasn't amused by this turn of events.

"How is it possible?" he growled, entering the security room at the Ministry. "Wasn't anyone guarding her?"

Samir followed him into the room, touching his wrist slightly with the tips of his fingers. The touch instantly calmed him, easing his frustration.

"There was, Your Majesty," an officer said, bowing to them. "I'm Officer Marrat, in charge of the investigation. The prisoner had outside help. Look." Turning to the numerous screens, he played one of the videos, enlarging it.

On the video, two men in hooded cloaks entered the corridor outside Dalatteya's cell. The three men guarding the cell turned sharply, reaching for their guns, but they halted, making strangled noises and grabbing their throats frantically, as if they were choking.

It seemed to be the taller of the two men's doing: he stepped forward, his hand clenched. The guards were losing consciousness one by one.

Warrehn frowned, watching the scene. Something tugged at his memory, and it took him a moment to remember why this seemed familiar. Eridan had such a talent too—the talent to choke people with his will when he was angry.

It was an extremely rare telepathic gift, but the man doing it definitely wasn't Eridan: he was tall, his hooded dark cloak failing to hide the breadth of his shoulders and his muscular build. Something about his posture was vaguely familiar to Warrehn, but he couldn't quite put his finger on it.

"Are they dead?" The other hooded man said. Warrehn recognized his voice. It was Uriel.

"Does it matter?" his companion said, taking a key card from the guard and opening the cell. He entered it, Uriel following him in.

"One moment," Officer Marrat said, switching to another camera.

This one showed Dalatteya in her cell.

She was seated on her bed in a plain prison uniform, her long, luscious hair a stark contrast to the gray dullness of her surroundings. She was staring at the floor blankly, her face pale and her eyes shiny with tears.

Samir inhaled sharply, emanating distress.

Warrehn took his hand. Samir exhaled, leaning his shoulder against Warrehn's. Officer Marrat glanced at them curiously, but looked away when Warrehn gave him a flat look.

On the video, the cell's door opened and Dalatteya lifted her gaze. Her mouth fell open as she stared at the hooded man.

"I'm sorry, my lady," Uriel said quickly, stepping into the cell, too. "I know I defied your orders, but I didn't know what else to do! I was pursued by the authorities and barely managed to get to the safe house. He convinced me that he could help me free you."

Slowly, Dalatteya got to her feet. And then her face crumpled and she was *running* toward the hooded man.

He caught her and hugged her tightly, her small body disappearing in the folds of his dark cloak.

"What in the world..." Samir whispered, staring at the scene in puzzlement. "Who is that?"

Warrehn shared his confusion.

But then he stiffened, eyeing the man's back as a suspicion formed in his mind. It seemed too outlandish, but...

"Is there another camera view?" he said hoarsely. "Show me the man's face."

"One moment, Your Majesty," Officer Marrat said, entering some commands into the terminal.

The video flickered, showing a view of Dalatteya's back.

"Shh, you're all right, my heart," the man said, stroking her back gently. He lifted his head from her hair, his blue eyes flashing with cold determination. "I will not let anyone touch you."

Samir sucked in a breath. Warrehn stared at the man's face.

"That's..." Officer Marrat said faintly.

Warrehn sighed, considering the implications of it. "It seems you were right," he said, squeezing Samir's fingers. "Your mother did love him, after all."

Samir nodded, watching his mother cling to the man she had claimed to hate—the man who was supposed to be dead.

"Have you managed to find their whereabouts?" Warrehn said, looking at Officer Marrat.

The man winced and said, "No. It's inexplicable. They should have been caught on the cameras after leaving the building, but it's like they disappeared into thin air. But not to worry, Your Majesty, I have all t-chambers, TNIT modules, and spaceports on high alert. Should they attempt to use any form of transport, they'll be arrested at once."

Warrehn shook his head.

Samir looked at him. "You don't believe they'll be caught?"

Smiling humorlessly, Warrehn pulled him out of the room. "We're dealing with a clone of Emyr'ngh'zaver," he said wryly. "One who has all his memories and abilities."

"And?" Samir said, looking confused.

"My father and I have never been close," Warrehn said, walking toward the nearest t-chamber. "He never had time for me when I was a child. But I remember the sole occasion he sat me down and taught me politics. And you know what his lesson was? That I should always think ahead and have contingency plans accounting for every possibility, no matter how unlikely." He snorted softly, wondering if Emyr had accounted for his precious Dalatteya killing him and then backtracking and giving him a cloned body when she had realized that she couldn't live without their toxic relationship. "I have little doubt that he will be able to get them off the planet. Knowing him, I would be surprised if he hadn't accounted for the possibility of Dalatteya being arrested and his existence being discovered."

"You're very calm about this," Samir said, looking at him with confusion and curiosity in his gaze as they entered the t-chamber.

"Fifth Royal Palace, west wing," Warrehn told the computer after verifying his identity. "I'm not calm," he said as they arrived. He stroked Samir's wrist with his thumb. "I guess I'm relieved."

"Relieved?" Samir said, following him out of the t-chamber into their palace.

Warrehn pulled him close. "Yes," he said, nuzzling Samir's cheek. Fuck, he smelled so good. "I still think your mother must answer for her crimes—it's only right—but I don't want you to be unhappy because of her, either. This way, it's out of my hands. Whatever happens, happens. Maybe Emyr's clone and Dalatteya will be arrested tomorrow. Or maybe they'll settle on some paradise planet and live their fucked-up version of happily ever after. Either way, it's out of our hands. It's oddly freeing." He pulled back to look Samir in the eyes. "We can be just us, without our parents' baggage and messy past."

Samir's expression became softer. "Just us?" he said in a tone of wonder, his long eyelashes fluttering as he blinked.

Fuck, he was so endearing. So damn lovely. Warrehn could look at him all day long. Now he understood Emyr's single-minded obsession with Dalatteya. He felt like his feelings for Samir could quickly twist into a toxic obsession that destroyed everything else if he couldn't have him—or had to share him with another man. The mere thought was sickening. No, he wouldn't let it happen.

"Just us," Warrehn said and kissed him.

Samir was smiling against his lips. "I love you," he whispered, looping his arms around Warrehn's neck.

Warrehn had known that already. He had felt it in their merge. But hearing it made his heart feel too big for his chest. It was such a strange, foreign feeling: happiness. He'd forgotten what it felt like.

"Marry me," he said.

Samir blinked, his lips parting in surprise. Then, he laughed, his eyes *sparkling*. "You're moving a little too fast, Your Majesty, don't you think?"

Not fast enough.

Warrehn pulled him closer. "I see no point in waiting. I will not let anyone else have you. We might as well make it official."

Samir chuckled. "You're impossible. That's not how things are done in our society."

"I don't care."

Laughing, Samir rolled his eyes. "I'm well aware of that. I'm sure Queen Kadira has never been dismissed from the room until she met you."

He was so beautiful when he laughed.

"Is that a no?" Warrehn said, wanting to kiss him again.

Samir's laugh turned into a gentle smile. "It should have been, but you must have rubbed off on me, you impossible man."

Warrehn hugged him tightly, burying his face in Samir's neck. He breathed deeply, trying to get a grip on his emotions. It almost felt like he was too happy, that this was too good to be true. Good things didn't happen, not to him. There was an irrational fear that this would be taken away from him, too.

"You make me feel too much," he said into Samir's neck. "It scares the shit out of me." Because he didn't know what he would have done if Samir said he wouldn't marry him, if Samir wasn't his to love, if Samir's bondmate had still been alive. He wanted to think he was a better man than his father, but… The truth was, he didn't know. What Emyr had done to Dalatteya and her husband was sickening, but Warrehn wasn't sure he would be any better if he had to watch Samir with another man. And it scared him. Maybe Dalatteya had been right, after all. Maybe the men of his family really were too toxic and obsessive.

He felt Samir's fingers in his hair, stroking it gently. "Look at me, War."

He lifted his head.

Samir's eyes were so very gentle as he took Warrehn's hand and entwined their fingers. "No one will take me away. I'm yours. I'll never leave you—I don't want to ever leave you." He smiled, squeezing Warrehn's fingers. "We've already established I'm the clingy one in this relationship."

It would have been embarrassing to be so transparent, but there was no judgment in Samir's gaze: only understanding and love.

Warrehn leaned forward and kissed him hard, pouring his emotions into it. *I want you, I need you, I love you.*

When they finally broke the kiss, they just gazed at each other for a moment before Samir grinned. "Let's go shock Ayda, shall we? She's going to yell at us."

"You mean, at you," Warrehn said, chuckling. "I'm the king. She can't yell at me."

Samir laughed. "Wanna bet?"

Warrehn snorted and said nothing, content to listen and watch his lovely face as Samir speculated about Ayda's reaction.

Warrehn knew it wouldn't be so easy. When the news about Dalatteya hit the press, they were going to be under a lot of scrutiny, Samir more than him. The last thing they needed was to invite more of it if they married soon. His PR team would no doubt have a lot to say on the subject. While normally Warrehn wouldn't give a fuck about people's opinions, he didn't want Samir to be ostracized for the things his mother had done, so he was prepared to listen to Ayda's advice on this.

If she told him to wait with the marriage, he would wait. He would do far more than that to protect what was his.

"You're quiet," Samir said, looking back at him. "What are you thinking about?"

"You," Warrehn said honestly.

Samir's answering smile was the most beautiful thing he'd ever seen. "Who are you and what happened to my moody, grumpy Warrehn?"

Warrehn thought back to the bitter, miserable man who had arrived at the palace all those months ago. He felt like a different man altogether.

"You happened," he said simply, pulling him close. Fuck, he couldn't hold him close enough.

Samir beamed at him. "I knew you were a closeted sap," he said, and kissed him.

Warrehn was smiling as he kissed back.

Maybe good things did happen to him.

Very good things.

The End

Bonus Content

The planet had four moons.

Sinking onto the couch on the patio, Dalatteya looked at the night sky. The view was quite beautiful, she had to admit. She'd had misgivings about settling on a planet that was part of the Union, even if it was a Fringe planet, but Emyr hadn't budged: he was too much of a creature of comfort to take residence on a pre-TNIT planet without any links to civilization. Dalatteya hadn't exactly been eager to give up access to GlobalNet, either, so she hadn't fought him hard on this, no matter her unease.

But it had been a year, and no one had found them yet. Perhaps Emyr was right and the planet was remote enough for its people not to care about some Calluvian outlaws. Either way, she had learned to appreciate this planet.

The sound of footsteps made her tense up before she recognized them and relaxed.

He settled on the couch next to her and slung his arm around her shoulders, nuzzling the side of her face. "Stargazing?" he murmured.

She hummed, leaning into him. She hated how much she craved his touch, but given the circumstances, it probably wasn't surprising. He was all she had, now that her son was beyond her reach.

The worst part was, part of her felt perfectly content with him being her entire world and her being his. *That's how it should be*, a voice whispered at the back of her mind.

Dalatteya tried to crush it. She didn't want to lose herself in him completely. She didn't trust Emyr at all, especially since he'd shown how crafty, resourceful, and manipulative he could be even when he'd been locked up with his telepathy limited. Now he walked this planet as a free man, coming and going as he pleased. She had no idea what he was up to when he left their seaside house for his trips to the nearest city. It unsettled her. And it unsettled her that she couldn't seem to breathe properly until he returned.

Gods, she despised herself sometimes. She needed something else to occupy her, before she could become completely dependent on him. More dependent than she already was.

"I have news," he said, handing her his multi-device.

Frowning, Dalatteya turned the screen on and inhaled sharply.

"I must say it isn't the way I thought we'd have grandchildren," Emyr said dryly. "But at least my eldest inherited my excellent taste, at least where looks are concerned."

She stared at her son in the picture. Samir's wrist was tied to Warrehn's with a ribbon, and they were smiling at each other. It was unmistakable what the picture depicted even without the headline proclaiming that King Warrehn'ngh'zaver had married Prince Samir'ngh'lavette.

Dalatteya pursed her lips, unsure what to feel. On one hand, she didn't like Warrehn, and she loathed the thought that the man who was the reason she was a fugitive had become Samir's spouse.

On the other hand, she was relieved that her son's future was now secured. Dalatteya was well aware that the scandal around her had hurt Samir's political standing by association. So, objectively, this was good news.

Subjectively, she felt more than a little heartbroken that she wasn't present at her only child's wedding and likely would never meet Samir's children. Perhaps it was her punishment. Perhaps she deserved it.

Sighing, Emyr pulled her tighter against him. "This self-flagellation doesn't suit you, Latteya."

"A mother is allowed to have regrets when she can't attend her only child's wedding."

Emyr hummed noncommittally and laid a proprietary hand on her stomach. "He isn't going to be the only child for much longer."

She froze, and then whipped her head toward him.

His blue eyes were smiling. "I'm surprised you haven't realized it yourself."

Dalatteya swallowed, her mind racing. "That's—that's—How do you know?" Her periods had been very irregular in the past few years until they finally stopped completely more than a year ago—or so she had assumed.

"I can feel her already," Emyr said with a soft smile. "Can't you?"

Her?

Dalatteya felt a burst of elation—and then a wave of crushing despair. "We can't have a child when we're both wanted criminals," she said hoarsely, closing her eyes. "I will not have my child grow up in such circumstances, forever living in fear of being caught and her parents taken away."

"Dalatteya. Look at me."

She opened her eyes.

Emyr's gaze was deadly serious as he said, "I will not let any harm come to either of you."

She shivered, believing him instinctively and loathing herself for it. She opened her mouth to say that he couldn't give such a promise, but he laid a finger on her lips, stopping her. "Our child will not have to live in fear. I have made all the arrangements." He retrieved two chips out of his pocket.

Dalatteya's breath caught. "Is that…?"

"It is," Emyr said, studying the chips with a satisfied gleam in his eyes. "Idhron has finally arranged new identities for us. As of today, we're law-abiding citizens of this planet."

She stiffened. "Idhron? And why is the High Adept of the High Hronthar helping us break the law?"

Emyr sighed, looking away before looking back at her with a placating expression. "Just remember to stay calm, all right, pet? You need to think of the baby."

Dalatteya glared at him. "Emyr. What. Did. You. Do?"

"Idhron found out about my existence years ago when he attempted to brainwash you into liking Eridan and came across the mind traps in your mind. He grew suspicious and had you followed to the safe house. Your security measures kept him away for a while, but eventually he compelled you into letting him into the house. You don't remember that because he wiped the relevant memories."

Dalatteya took a deep breath and counted to ten. "And then?"

"We talked," Emyr said, looking at her warily. "He realized what I am, but he obviously saw little benefit in informing the authorities of my existence. I was living proof of your crimes if he ever needed to get rid of you politically, but he also realized that I was more useful as an ally. I agreed to let him brainwash you into liking Eridan and I have given him a lot of blackmail material against the other royal families in exchange for a favor I would collect on some day."

"You—I can't believe you!" Dalatteya shoved him away and sprang to her feet. "You let him brainwash me? You despicable scumbag—"

Emyr stood up too, having the nerve to look exasperated. "Darling, calm down—"

She smacked him across his stupidly handsome face, hating him, loathing him utterly, and then attempted to smack him again, but he yanked her close, pulling her flush against him.

"I did it to protect you," he snarled. "You were too self-confident, too careless, Latteya. You were always going to get caught, sooner or later, and I knew we'd need a contingency plan for that. The deal I made with Idhron is the reason we escaped Calluvia so easily and the reason we have brand new identities so we can live without constantly looking over our shoulders." He held her gaze. "When Idhron found me, I could have left with him. I didn't. I stayed there for you."

She huffed, but most of her anger left. "And what, am I supposed to believe Idhron will keep his end of the deal out of the goodness of his heart? If he knows our new identities, he will have us arrested at a moment's notice!"

"He won't," Emyr said, stroking her back. His eyes became colder, harder. "He knows that if he betrays us, I will expose the High Hronthar for what it is. I gave Uriel the proof and where to go with it in case we're arrested or killed."

She stared at him. She had been so angry when Emyr had told her in no uncertain terms that her loyal bodyguard couldn't stay with them. She had thought it was just a power play, to show that now he was the one making the decisions. She'd never entertained the thought that Uriel's leaving was truly necessary.

"All right," she said, her shoulders sagging. "But you're still a bastard, and I still despise you."

"Mhm," Emyr said, pressing their foreheads together and smiling his insufferably attractive smile. "And I still love you dearly, my darling."

She scoffed, but it was half-hearted. She knew he loved her, loved her more than anything, in his own twisted, unhealthy way. Had he not loved her, he never would have forgiven her for what she'd done. And had she not loved him back, she would never have forgiven him, either.

Perhaps their love was toxic, unhealthy, and messed-up, but it was *theirs*. And she could never give it up. She was done living in denial. She couldn't live without him. She had tried. She had. For all of four days before creating him a new body.

She hated this feeling, hated the strength of it, but without it, she was nothing. She both hoped Samir didn't love Emyr's son as intensely as she loved Emyr and pitied him if he didn't. If Samir didn't know such love, he'd never feel the utter emptiness she felt when Emyr had died, but he also wouldn't know the soul-wrenching perfection of being in the arms of the man she loved.

"Let's go inside," she whispered, kissing Emyr desperately, her heart clenching at the memory of his dead, mutilated body.

She ran her hands over his wide, strong back. He was alive. He was here. He would never leave her alone and hollow again. Even if he died, she would revive him again and again, until the end of time, until the universe was nothing but a void.

"Same," Emyr said hoarsely, reading her thoughts through their bond. He embraced her so tightly it bordered on painful. "Until the end of time."

The End

About the Author

Alessandra Hazard is the author of the bestselling MM romance series *Straight Guys, The Wrong Alpha, Calluvia's Royalty*.

Visit Alessandra's website to learn more about her books: http://www.alessandrahazard.com/books/

To be notified when Alessandra's new books become available, you can subscribe to her mailing list: http://www.alessandrahazard.com/subscribe/

You can contact the author at her website or email her at author@alessandrahazard.com.